ALSO BY LEA CARPENTER

Eleven Days

red, white, blue

red
white
blue

LEA
CARPENTER

Alfred A. Knopf
NEW YORK
2018

Library of Congress Cataloging-in-Publication Data
Names: Carpenter, Lea, author.
Title: Red, white, blue : a novel / Lea Carpenter.
Description: First edition. | New York : Alfred A. Knopf, 2018.
Identifiers: LCCN 2017047883 | ISBN 9781524732141 (hardcover) |
ISBN 9781524732158 (ebook)
Subjects: | GSAFD: Suspense fiction.
Classification: LCC PS3603.A7698 R43 2018 | DDC 813/.6—dc23
LC record available at https://lccn.loc.gov/2017047883

Jacket photograph: My Good Images/Shutterstock
Jacket design by Jenny Carrow

Manufactured in the United States of America
First Edition

This book is for the extraordinary people
who shared their stories with me.

The structure of the difficulty begins to disclose itself. We cannot construct an explanation. We do not know which of our facts are bricks and which are papier-mâché painted to look like bricks. We can only watch the way the bricks are handled. It is painful, nonetheless, to relinquish one's hope for a narrative, to admit that the study of the CIA may not lead to the exposure of facts so much as to the epistemology of facts. We will not get the goods so quickly as we will learn how to construct a model which will tell us why we cannot get the goods.

—NORMAN MAILER, "A Harlot High and Low"

Contents

grace

Grace. She had inherited it though it can be learned. She was, some might say, born for public life. She was also born temperamentally disposed against it, against even the occasional party. She found parties both stressful and boring. Not many things qualify as at once stressful and boring. Taxes. Waiting. As a child she was the envy of other mothers who interpreted her reserve as manners. As a girl she was the one who shared her Halloween candy with strangers. And at Princeton, she distinguished herself by studying Chinese (her father said it was essential, to understand the world) and Russian (her mother said it was essential, to read the novels). She also distinguished herself by moving off campus with a senior when she was a freshman. And while it might have looked from the outside as if her time there was spent mainly in libraries, it was mainly spent falling in love. That senior graduated and moved away. Three years later, Anna graduated, too. Summa cum laude, Phi Beta Kappa, absolutely no clue.

red

Espionage is not a math problem.

When we met, your father told me about the night you were born, how he spent it in a hospital but not with you and your mother, in a hospital in a city far away from the one where you arrived, on time. He said, with that sly charm, "Though where I was wasn't quite a hospital, in truth. It wasn't quite a city, either." He described looking out the window and seeing fires in the streets. He described thinking about your name while watching his friend die, the blood on his hands. His friend, his colleague.

He told me they'd chosen "Anna" finally, not because of the literary echoes but because your mother had liked its lyricism, the precision of those twin A's on either end. Precision, or was it simplicity? He said, "And also because the letter A is a beginning, and I wanted to remember that night as being about the start of something rather than about an end." I didn't say that the letter A always made me think of endings, as in answers, as in questions and answers. The answers are what matter.

I met your father within the first hour of my first day at the Agency. He told me that story, then took me to see the stars on the wall, each star linked to a loss of life. He pointed to one and said, "That was my friend the night she was born, in that hospital in that city with those fires." He told me he planned to take you to see the star when you were old enough.

I didn't understand at the time what he was talking about. I went into this for the thrill, the mission, the risk. Some boys want to be quarterback. I wanted something different. Your father was trying to tell me that the essence of the experience would be emotional. "Espionage isn't a math problem," he said. Espionage is intimacy, a trip to the truth. I was a skilled interrogator, but the hardest interrogation is the one we perform on ourselves, of course. Your father always said, "Ask the hard questions." And, "Write down the answers, else you'll forget."

These are my answers. This is what happened, and why, what I know and believe. This story doesn't involve fires, though it does involve a goddess or two. It does involve a dying friend. It involves a young officer who followed orders and committed crimes and fell in love and saved a life.

I believe in forgiveness.

I believe except the Lord keep the city, the watchman will wake, but in vain.

I believe in you.

This is the story of your father, Anna. You are old enough now.

white

An avalanche can be triggered by weather or surface conditions. It can be triggered by a single skier's slip. Even an expert can be caught in an avalanche. And the most common cause of death in this case is asphyxiation. It's a kind of drowning, actually, drowning in snow. When her father died in an avalanche, Anna became obsessed with mountain weather, with snow. She learned that in the winter of 1951, also called the Winter of Terror, there were 649 avalanches in the Alps alone, that more than ninety lost their lives in the canton of Valais, in Switzerland, which is exactly where her father had a home and where he hiked to find fresh tracks the day he died, sixty some winters later. After she buried him near the Matterhorn, Anna had her own Winter of Terror. She was newly married and living, as one friend put it, "in the mourning shell, an Athenian isolation tank of loss." *Shell, tank*—that sounded about right. And yet just as she was most focused on herself and on her own pain, someone presented her with a problem even more complex than loss. The effect of this was what one might call empathy, or perspective. One might also call it *deus ex machina*. Anna met this guy with his problem at Cap d'Antibes, in the South of France, only seven months after placing edelweiss on her father's Swiss grave. He would pull her out of the tank, soaking and alive.

one

Q.

A.

Do you know about spectral evidence? Did he ever talk to you about spectral evidence, from the witch trials. He talked to me about it. The trials were one of his absolute obsessions. Spectral evidence, declared inadmissible by Increase Mather, 1692, was central to those prosecutions. Increase, Cotton's father, president of Harvard, a serious person, a man of God, a man who believed in the importance of young men learning Greek, who believed in human kindness, who believed in his New World. Who believed in order. And who denied the viability of spectral evidence, despite Cotton's strong claims in its favor. Spectral evidence was testimony, a witness's recollection of a vision or dream in which she was assaulted by a witch. Dreams and visions were presented, and received, as fact during those trials, presided over by a court designed for the exclusive purpose of sorting the witch situation. Increase Mather knew spectral evidence was specious. God, Ancient Greek, and political prudence—that was Increase. The devil can assume many shapes, was his view. Who's to say visions aren't planted in the minds of the victims, was his view. Perhaps it wasn't a witch at all who visited those girls, perhaps it was simply adolescent imagination. Or desire. This position was a hedge, though, a way not to question the existence of witches while urging prosecutorial logic. In my view. One might wonder whether you can kill a witch, yes, but the executions placed an anxious people at ease. "Molestations from the invisible world," is what Cotton Mather called the crimes. Increase later wrote that "it were better that ten suspected witches should escape, than that one innocent person should be condemned." Some things are elegant in theory, Anna, but bloody in practice. Like believing in witches. Or evil.

Rebel.

Where did it come from, that sense Anna had of herself as being different from her peers. She wasn't sure. It had always been there. It wasn't arrogance. It might have been fear. She had always felt a longing for risk in her life, having been born into a part of the world that could feel absolutely riskless, a place that appeared to be defined by traditions, order, and rule. Though those traditions and rules served a purpose, like crenellated castle walls. They were there in anticipation of enemy fire. Traditions tell us what to do but order tells us what not to do. The what-not-to's: These were Anna's problem. That perfect grace of the child she once was would be eclipsed by the perfect rebellion of an adolescent who dazzled teachers in her days but stayed out too late nights, trying on different levels of risk. And this unexpected element in her character would lead to choices that did set her apart. That instinct to rebel is what led her to the most important choices she would make—whom to love, whom to trust. As she grew older and started to encounter experiences she could not possibly control, Anna learned to keep her less practical instincts caged, damp the rebel. But the rebel will always out. During high school she would wander into her father's office on nights he was home and ask questions like, "What do you do with all your rage." "Oh, you embrace it," he would say, smiling as if this answer were obvious. He would lean back in his chair like he owned the world, which at one point she believed he did. He called her moods "dark and stormies," and told her to welcome them. He didn't believe in therapy. He believed all the help we ever need is within us. This was his ethos. It was what drew him to Asia—that cultural discipline, precision. And that instinct to always take the long view.

Q.
A.

The polygraph is a very elaborate parlor trick. Studies have been run, and they always come back with this or that point about efficacy. Levels of efficacy. People confuse "efficacy" and "utility," though. Your chance of detecting deception on a poly is no better than that, chance. Why don't you just have a guy who has a coin. And that's really all they have, Anna.

After they go through their questions they leave the room. Then they come back in and say something like, *I really want to help you through this,* and they add something like, *I know you are having trouble with one of these questions.* Then they take a dramatic pause and say, *Which one do* you *think it is?* They're trained. They're taught about the pause.

It takes less training to become a polygrapher in the state of Virginia than it takes to become a cosmetologist. I really looked at the whole history of this, after everything happened. They're charlatans. They're kids who come in and they can ruin careers. They can do it for any reason. They can do it for no reason. They can do it because they've had a bad day. And they will skew the tests. Yes, the tests are skewable. There is an element of time, too—the length of the polygraph itself, and the length of time you're left waiting to hear. It's called polygraph limbo, that time when you're waiting to hear what the results are, if there was "deception indicated" or not. People are left in limbo for weeks, months. At any one time there are a number of people Langley cannot clear and they cannot fire, according to their own policies. Does that sound efficient to you. Does that sound like efficacy.

Angleton was the start of that culture. The counterespionage folks constitute a small group within the Counterintelligence Center, not exactly a center of excellence in my opinion. I mean, if you can't gather intelligence, you're put in counterintelligence, like Putin. If you're a star they want you out on the street, shaking down Russians or Yemenis or, as was the case in my case, Chinese. If you're a star you don't sit at a desk. At least not a counterintelligence desk. These were the dumbest people at the Agency with the exception of the people in security.

They do have a silver bullet. Or perhaps I should call it the absence of a bullet. They don't have the burden of proof. They have no standard. You are guilty as charged because they feel you're guilty as charged. A polygraph is a Rorschach test, Anna. A polygraph is a hammer in search of a nail. Like the Bavarian Illuminati, the absence of proof becomes proof itself. If you're under suspicion, you're under suspicion. *Sic erat scriptum.* Only there is no script.

Once the poly is complete it's sent to Quality Control. Yes, "quality control," for a coin flip at the circus.

They don't let you leave believing you passed. You're supposed to leave that room, return home, panic, then come back and tell them all the things you thought about overnight. Come back and confess. I remember one conversation. It went like this:

POLYGRAPHER: Why don't you respect this process?
    ME: I've read the literature.
POLYGRAPHER (horrified): Why did you read the
        literature?
    ME: I don't know—I want to be educated?
POLYGRAPHER: I don't understand.
    ME: Exactly.

For a long time I thought that all that this problem needed was a little adult supervision. I was wrong. I had a close friend in the general counsel's office, a serious attorney, Yale Law and all that. Some of those attorneys process the polygraphs. They also see the admissions, some made under the duress of the poly, some given freely. And there are serious admissions. You know, so-and-so was in Vietnam and threw a kid out of a helicopter. That's a serious admission. Admitting you had dinner with a Chinese girl once during your tour in Asia is not a serious admission. But these are people who have likely known China only via eating spring rolls at Tysons Corner. So what do they know. Throw a kid from a helicopter. Think about that. There is a spectrum of serious and there is a spectrum of crime. The process of the poly explodes and mocks these spectrums.

The person who invented the polygraph is William Marston, whose other great achievement in life was writing the *Wonder Woman* cartoons. Do you remember her magic golden lasso of truth. We're talking about magic lassos. We're talking about you, in a freezing room, in this high-backed chair with tubes strapped on to you. When I asked them, "What are you looking for," their response was, "You're not adequately respecting this process."

I find it interesting that when a theory of enhanced interrogations was required, no one called in the polygraphers. Though I shouldn't say that. That's not adequately respecting the process, is it. Your father only wanted to do the right thing, which in my case was saving a life.

Koan.

Anna learned from her father that the word *koan* came from the Chinese. He explained how it was a compound of two characters: the character 公—public, official, governmental, common, collective, fair, equitable; and the character 案—table, desk, case as in law case, record, file, plan, proposal. It amused him that what one might misread as *governmental plan* or *official record* was a thing neither certain nor clear. "Plans and records tell us what will happen, or what has happened," he would say. He loved the idea of koans, that they are questions posing as riddles, questions not designed to teach by providing answers but rather by freeing a mind, by provoking doubt and confusion. "Why do I need to provoke doubt and confusion" Anna would ask. "I'm a teenage girl—I'm already mired in all that." On the night before her college graduation, the koans came up again. They'd gone for ice cream at the local place—her father always asked for vanilla in a sugar cone. They'd walked back to her dorm and into her room, which was empty except for the bed, and boxes. Looking at the boxes, she teased her father, "I feel doubt and confusion are provoking me."

Even then she knew certainty isn't any more useful than that summa cum laude. Doubt, now we're talking. Her father had put his arm around her which was his way of saying he understood. She would have liked to stay academic after school, but life intervened. After school she was living at home, sleeping in her childhood bed, and eating alone most nights. She wasn't making any money and felt anxious about that though her father would always say, "Money's not the metric," by which he meant the metric for a life deeply lived. Depth is elusive in your early twenties, and Anna was no exception. Everything at that time felt temporary and light. And yet she was changing. She was growing out of the girl she had been, out of optimism. Studying Russian novels or koans had once struck her as serious. Later these things would strike her as silly. Literature, ha. Enlightenment, Anna would tell her twenty-two-year-old self, employed at the Ford Foundation, how absurd. In this way she was growing, yes, but she was also letting go of something she perhaps wasn't even aware she once had: faith in herself. It was only much later that Anna welcomed faith back and in doing so finally understood what the metric is.

Q.

A.

There's terrorism and there's long-term strategic interests. Some might say fighting terrorists is a clearer game, with a more immediately identifiable set of risks and rewards. Others will argue espionage in essence is about the long-range, about understanding enemies operating on a different clock. It's chess versus checkers. Your father preferred chess.

China is the second-largest economy now, and gaining. Soon they will overtake us in everything. Even though it'll be a while, they'll eventually also overtake us in technological capabilities. The time it will take for that depends on how much they can steal, and how quickly. We say they're trailing us, yes, but you see they can simply steal what's new. Morality is a different concept to them. They're not Catholic. They don't have guilt. It's almost imperative, in their view, to steal to get ahead, especially from foreigners. I am talking about a people I love. I am talking about a country I love. I am talking about a service I admire. If you have empathy, you can understand. It's a question of culture.

red, white, blue

. . .

Chinese intelligence describes itself as having a "thousand grains of sand" philosophy. What does American intelligence do when it wants to know what the beach at Cap d'Antibes is like. It enlists the National Reconnaissance Office to take and study satellite images of the Mediterranean. It orders the National Security Agency to bug phone calls coming to and from the area. CIA sends in a human agent, he or she walks around, eats a crepe, speaks to surfers. The navy commands a sub to troll the coast.

If Chinese intelligence wants to know what the beach at Cap d'Antibes is like, they send a thousand tourists there. "Tourists." Each tourist collects a single grain of sand. Then those tourists return to China, and Chinese intelligence rebuilds that beach, at their base, one grain at a time.

The China Ops course takes place in a little white house on the Langley grounds. It's exclusive. Say we have a case officer in Africa who's beginning to develop a Chinese asset. CIA will invite that officer home and he can spend a few days in that house learning how to recruit a Chinese official. You're not learning tricks, really. It's more of an emotional, cultural education. You often have the Old Wise Men, senior officers working in China, come and talk. It's cerebral, and not boring. In an office like China Ops, there's no sharing or trust; it's hard to learn. The little white house was an exception to that. There, people opened up. People talked about their lives and conversations had a different depth. That house is where I learned about the grains of sand. It's where I listened to a lecture on Chinese prison protocols, delivered by your father. He knew some things. And he always cut the hard parts with humor.

. . .

We were taught about the Chinese "century of humiliation," how even during the founding of the Communist Party, millions of Chinese died. We learned how in the eighties, China started to get its shit together and now she's riding high. Look at a map. Hong Kong. Macau. Taiwan, soon. They have border disputes with every single one of their neighbors. Every truck you see in Africa is Chinese. That's soft power. Now they're in talks to build a base in Afghanistan, the Middle East, think about that. They have one aircraft carrier, the United States has eleven. Eleven isn't so many more than one.

Americans may have the idea of being American, but not in the same way the Chinese have the idea of being Chinese. There are people who identify as Chinese who haven't been to China for generations. Go to Vietnam, or Malaysia. You'll find a lot of leaders in those places who self-identify as Chinese, and that has implications. My family originally came from Scotland but if someone said, "Hey, we'd like you to spy for Scotland," I'd tell them to fuck off. Imagine a nation at once aggressive and untested militarily. Picture a child with a gun. Wait, a child with a nuclear weapon. This seems to me like a huge strategic problem. I mean, larger than guys running around Iraq and Syria waving black flags.

Asia is interesting and important to CIA for a number of reasons. Malaysia was the place where all the key 9/11 hijackers met before the attacks. Indonesia was the place where the majority of Al Qaeda bombings, through its regional affiliate, Jemaah Islamiyah, took place in the early 2000s. And let's not forget North Korea. I'd define a thirty-year-old with an atomic bomb as a problem, not that age is always correlated with wisdom. Kissinger was barely forty when he served as foreign policy adviser to the Rockefeller campaign. Kissinger understood China. He knew China would never be a case of *Here comes another bomb plot—let's put measures in place to prevent it;* the Chinese don't think that way. To understand someone else you must see her as she sees you. To understand China you must see her as she sees you. Kissinger understands the answer to the question What does a problem look like when it cooks for a decade, or three, rather than an hour. It looks like the South China Sea.

Buddhists.

In her early thirties, Anna attended the wedding of a family friend in Klosters. The groom was a young British filmmaker who had spent time finding himself after Oxford, and when he found himself he found religion, too. He had become a Buddhist. The bride seemed fine with that, and no one pressed back on what it really meant. The dinner following the ceremony, which had taken place in the small, stone village church, was on top of the mountain. Guests had to ride the gondola up, and while it was June, it was cold, and boys were offering girls blazers. The best man, who definitely wasn't Buddhist, offered his to Anna. It was almost dark by the time everyone reached the top, where there were waiters in a long line as they exited the cars, each waiter holding a roll of colored fabric to offer to the guests. Unfurled, those rolls revealed themselves to be Bhutanese prayer flags. Anna watched as her old friends tied flags to a wire the bride had had suspended from two chairlift poles, her gift to the groom. "To bless the marriage," she told people. Though even absent the blessing, the visual effect was stunning. Everyone angled iPhones to catch the colors against the light. Anna's father put his arm around her and she remembered thinking he was going to say something about marriage, something about one day her prince would come, or maybe even something about her mother, who wasn't there, who hadn't been there in some time, speaking of prayers. Instead he said, "Belief isn't for the faint of heart." He wasn't mocking the flags exactly, he was stating a case. Anna didn't go home that night with her father she went home with the best man who was roguish and drunk so in the morning, over late croissants, her father expressed concern about her choices. This was becoming a talk they had regularly, as she entered the era when everything was seen through the lens of finding a future, and a family.

"Only, the thing is, I knew," she said, deflecting, as if knowing made it acceptable, or painless. "I knew what I was doing."

The hotel's little breakfast room was filled with couples, ones who'd hooked up the night before which is to say ones who'd happily slept in. Anna imagined them all moving swiftly from flirtations and first kiss to a second then third child, haloed in the confidence that comes from getting it right. She had never had that confidence; she was chronically convinced she would never get it right, all evidence to the contrary. Which is perhaps why she so often threw the game.

"How are you," her father said, breaking the silence. They hadn't connected for a meal in some time; he'd been busy.

"I don't know, I think I am slightly tired of waiting."

"Waiting for what. One can't rush it," he said.

"Rush what, life?"

"Life, love. Cheese soufflé. You really can't rush anything."

"Yes, it's all marathons, not races, isn't it."

"Marathons, not *sprints,* darling. A marathon is a race," he said. She was looking at the best man, who sort of careened into the room without acknowledging her. He possessed that obscene yet casual pride only the really pretty ones can carry off. She looked at him but she spoke to her father.

"How do you always get it right. How do you always know?"

"When someone tells you who they are, you listen," he said. And then he looked at the best man, who was lighting a Marlboro in sly disregard for rule. "People usually tell you."

Within six months he would purchase the chalet in Switzerland and announce his intention to spend winters there. "Are you becoming a Buddhist," Anna would tease. For years, whenever she thought about Switzerland, she thought less about prayers and more about that breakfast, what they'd discussed, this idea that people tell you who they are. As of people, so of things: A thing can elicit emotion, too, can tell you what it is, and you should believe it when it tells you. Sometimes a thing looks like a riddle when it's a clue. The thing that arrived in Anna's mail after her father died, after the burial and the honeymoon, looked like a riddle but was actually a clue. It was trying to tell her something. You might say it was shouting.

Q.

A.

I thought it would be useful for my advancement to have studied in China, but the people in the Office of Security have the final say on everything that could count as a threat. They determine if and when you come or go, stay or leave. And they know that they won't ever really lose touch with you. They know that you know once you enter, you will be reporting back to them in ways for the rest of your life. You want to take a course on seventeenth-century poetry after you've left the Agency? Well, if you write a paper on John Donne that you want to publish in *The New York Review of Books,* you will have to submit a request.

Documents provide a record, of course. And in theory what we're recording is the truth. If it's not documented, it didn't happen. My favorite document is the "Unofficial Foreign Contact Report." Any foreigner with whom you have a *close and continual* relationship requires this form. *Close and continual* has a bit of a muddy definition but it's essentially anyone you are close to, or who has unescorted access to your house. A maid. A driver. A lover.

Q. A.

These reports are like vitamins, never at the top of your list. Though God forbid you come home and haven't filled them out properly, you're crucified. Whatever excuse you come up with is interpreted as a lie or a cover, which it may well be. Yes, it's ironic. We were in the business of learning to lie, only don't lie back to the Mothership. "Don't bait the Bavarian Illuminati," your father would say.

Heaven.

Inside the package she received after the avalanche, after the delayed honeymoon, Anna found a tiny silver USB she of course immediately opened. On it was a collection of videos, divided neatly into "chapters," each titled with one word. The first, "Rooms," opened with a little boy talking about Heaven and God. A voice-over, set against a black screen.

> *There is a room where you go and you can know that God exists. And there is a room where one knows that the sun always comes up. And also there is a room where one goes to die. A room where one rests after dying. And also there is a room where one goes to understand. And also there is a room, where one dies.*

This vision of Heaven was the exact vision of Heaven her father had once described to her. "If Heaven exists, what do you think it's like," she'd asked, after friends had gone partying and crashed their car and one was in critical condition.

"I think it's quite like a house," he said, with absolute confidence. "A very large house with many rooms."

"Tell me," she said.

He had gone on to talk about the rooms, how there is one for forgiveness, one for rest, even a room for joy. The joy room was vast. It contained a central courtyard floored with stone. "Joy needs her space," he had said. Anna often thought about that courtyard, which included hibiscus vines and bougainvillea, a magical glass trellis. He described how from this room, you could see all the way to the edge of the earth, to the sea. Her father had taught her many things, defined her views on literature, manners, God. And emotion. He had prepared her to expect a certain level of creativity, or romance, in relationships. Set her up to expect comfort when she felt in crisis. He knew clouds and angels weren't quite enough, when asked about Heaven. In this and other things, he set a bar.

That bar broke hearts. Anna's first love had been older and had taught her how to love. Her second became her husband and would teach her how to let go. There were others, each of whom would eventually mention her "high emotional bar." This always shocked Anna; *What bar,* she would say. Or, *What's your defini-tion of high.* She was unaware of measuring, even as she clung to her yardstick. She was unaware that her real understanding of love came not from university or from marriage but from her father. The game of measuring beaus against fathers is common and unfair. It's rigged against the beaus whose flaws we see clearly in favor of fathers whose flaws are obscured, or willfully hidden, in the presence of a child.

The last time Anna had used her yardstick was with the guy she met on her honeymoon, at the hotel by the ocean at the Cap. The honeymoon wasn't really a honeymoon, as it took place almost seven months after the wedding, but as it was their first real time away since exchanging vows, since burying her father, and her husband had been insistent about framing it that way. *Honeymoon, honeymoon:* He must have repeated the word ten times in the Air France departure lounge alone. "Can't we simply say holiday," she'd asked him. His enthusiasm made her shy, but his enthusiasm made him who he was, it was the center of his charm. He adored her and was proud of her, and he wanted to show off the celebration of that to anyone and everyone. "Holiday," she repeated, as they waited in line to board the plane. And he had picked her up, and looked her right in the eyes and said, "I love you. You are allowed to be happy." He had a point.

She'd started seeing a psychiatrist that summer and quickly concluded that everyone was seeing shrinks, hoping maybe more for forgiveness than epiphany. Anna sometimes fell asleep in her sessions, and the shrink said it was because in a "framework of safety" she could rest. She preferred the theory that talking about her problems bored her out of consciousness.

The trip would be a chance for rest, though. She could finally find the right time to tell her husband her news. He was busy these days, and absent, though he didn't mean it, it wasn't an active thing against her. He was preparing to sell his company, which he referred to as "the baby." He was the sole founder and owner and would tell people it had been "another case of Immaculate Conception." When they landed in Nice he got a text telling him the baby had been valued at a very heady number.

"What does that number mean," she'd asked.

"Freedom," was his answer, which she interpreted to mean he didn't know.

On their second day in France she was alone again in the afternoon while he worked, so she went to the bar. The only other person there was reading a book and eating olives. Later, he would claim that when she sat down he had asked, *"Lune de miel?"* the French phrase for honeymoon. He would also claim that she had answered shyly and in perfect French, "No, only holiday." Answering yes would have prompted questions about the wedding and elicited answers about the story, why the honeymoon hadn't followed the wedding, and then if she said what had happened, there would have been shock or sympathy. A little white lie was so much simpler.

Anna could recall only what she was wearing, a white eyelet dress found online. The necklace her father had given her for her thirtieth birthday, a gold pendant dotted with tiny blue stones, one for each of her years.

At the bar the guy had pushed a silver cup of peanuts toward her. She took two. "They import those from Georgia," he'd said, teasing, mocking the pretense of silver cups for such a simple thing as peanuts. Something in him had drawn her out. Something in him had made her feel calm. It wasn't physical or illicit. It was simple: He was listening. He was hearing her. She was telling him who she was and he was hearing it. Within an hour she was telling him about the wedding and the snow and the loss.

And also there is a room, where one dies.

At the end of the first chapter, the first video, the camera pans back and she can now see the boy. "What do you want to be when you grow up?" says a woman's voice.

The boy moves his face so close to the camera you can see only a blur.

"Superman," he says.

"What's so special about Superman?"

"He gets to save the world."

Q.

A.

Look, the average age of a first-tour operations officer is under thirty-five. You are sending many of these single—or let's call them "geographically single"—guys to foreign places. They will date local women. They're human. So the question always arises, *At what point do you fill out the report?* Your father liked to say, "You fill it out after five dinners, or two breakfasts. One breakfast, it's on the house." Though in my experience, there weren't many meaningful breakfasts. Meaningful breakfasts are an occupational hazard, and while no one writes down a list of those hazards, everyone knows what they are. It all goes back to paranoia and distrust. Paranoia and distrust, especially of foreigners—the exact same people we were sent over to befriend and seduce, befriend and betray. I remember once telling a new guy he needed to mind the reports, that they were "simple protocol." Your father was there and he said, "Protocol. Or, as we called it, survival."

When I started I had absolutely no idea about anything. I didn't know what the word *threat* meant. The definition, and the author of that definition, isn't disclosed at the Farm. Later, you learn. A threat is a situation that requires you to make an immediate decision, and the options usually aren't right choice and wrong choice. The options are usually complex choice and really complex choice. If you're blessed there's occasionally a third option: the "only one." The idea of only-one scenarios was explained to me at a bar one night, watching girls order drinks. One of the girls was particularly striking, less for beauty than for her height, rare in that part of the world. "That's an only-one scenario," someone said. When I asked what that meant he told me, "A situation where the only option is equally seductive and terrifying." Then he said, "You know, removal of a dictator, falling in love, equally seductive and terrifying." See how many things you can think of that fit into that category, Anna. Here is one: organizing the extradition of an asset to save her life while risking your own.

Space.

"Look at this tangle of thorns," her father would say, when he would find Anna in the kitchen, amid one of her messes. She'd loved cooking when she was a girl, and had devoured the recipe books her mother left behind—M.F.K. Fisher, Escoffier. He would find her at ten or eleven or twelve, the same child who grew up to be so controlled and meticulous, covered in flour surrounded by pots and cracked eggshells, the cook having indulged her by letting her loose. "My little act of creative destruction," he called her. Those nights her father would slip off his jacket and roll up his sleeves and join her. As she grew up they spent hours in that kitchen talking food and art and life. Anna couldn't recall many nights between ten and fifteen when he wasn't home. A girl's life is defined by school, family, eventually by boys, later motherhood. Her father's life was defined by her.

What else did Anna's mother leave behind? A legacy of taste, of how things should be and where one must travel, of what constitutes a proper hospital corner (even as she herself had never made a bed), and what the finest five-star hotels were in any city between Edinburgh and Istanbul. Her mother exemplified a kind of perfection other women tried, and failed, to crib. Though it wasn't so much the perfection that was her art—perfection being eminently crib-able—as it was the effortlessness that attended it. Anna's mother never broke a sweat, excepting on the tennis court. She sort of floated above.

She had gone to the right schools and married the right man. She had delivered a beautiful baby girl she would dress in smocked Spanish jumpers for outings in Central Park.

She was adored by everyone and seemed to bestow adoration democratically in response. Her most formidable gift was her ability to perform, and her finest performance was as the sine qua non of humility, that girl from a grand family who would never trade on it.

In private she could be wickedly subversive and even critical—of her peers, even of her husband, who had come from a very different world, and whom she loved more than he loved her. Wickedness comes from loneliness, though, and Anna's mother knew it. She knew that her long line of perfect performances had led her to a prison of her own design. A prison on Fifth Avenue, how absurd. Though that is how she felt. No one was going to rescue her. No one would have questioned her, as everyone felt she had the perfect life, right down to those smocked dresses and that little girl who would without question grow up to be like her mother, another thoroughbred. And so one day, tired of performing, she left.

She would tell herself her job was done. She would tell herself that she had given everything she had to her little girl, and that when there was nothing left to give . . . She would insist on a narrative about life in general which Anna spent a long time fighting and scorning, one that says we are always free to leave, that we have only ourselves to mind. That one must take risks. Ironically, this was not a narrative Anna's father believed in. Ironically, as he understood the concept of risk. He understood it so well he believed it should be confined to work, to math. When it came to private life he believed in duty and rule and precision. His narrative was that his wife had given up, that her entitlement had ruined her, that entitlement was a cancer. His narrative was that when you love something you give your life for it. At least, that was how Anna understood him. That was how she understood them both, and she had confidence in her understanding of who they were, as all children do. Later, when she was old enough to have confidence in her *own* choices, she would consider that understanding, those opposing narratives. She would have to choose one over the other.

Children intuit the emotions of their elders. They cue their own emotions off of those. Anna's mother possessed an even, chilly temperament. Her father was warm and intense. One might say, observing things, that if she had to lose one parent it might have been better to lose her mother. Though who can say. Anna would be raised well by a raft of other adults, Irish nannies, her father, his girlfriends. And in ways she would raise herself. Though a child doesn't really think about who is raising them. A child thinks about who is setting bedtimes, or selecting what goes under the tree. A child thinks adults are people who police and protect them. It doesn't occur to a child that what parents are trying to do is actually raise an adult. It doesn't occur to a child that parents are just trying to do the right thing. Like all those years later, all grown up in that bar on her "honeymoon," Anna was also only trying to do the right thing.

A man who quotes Nabokov apropos of cracked eggs: That was Noel. He'd studied English at Virginia, and stayed on for an MFA.

He'd met her mother at a party on the North Shore. He had ambitions to be a writer but was too poor to pursue poetry alone, so he went to Wall Street. That had worked out well for him, to his own amusement. It turned out that slant rhyme wasn't his only gift; he could also select stocks. He would forever refer to the financial world as "life at the putty-knife factory," though he rarely discussed his work. When she was little, Anna knew only that Noel did something involving math, and a commute below Fourteenth Street.

When he left the bank to start his own thing, his office was a walk-up with two desks and a water cooler. Later his office was a great glass box designed by a Pritzker Prize recipient. He'd met the architect at a dinner in London. He'd been seduced by the man's riffs on transparency, and the meaning of space. Thirty years after completing his dissertation at a diner in Charlottesville, Noel had become an icon. Though not as he had thought he might. Not as the new Lowell, or Merwin. He was a pillar in another field, in demand for another kind of virtuosic talent. He could value things, and by that point not just stocks. He could accurately assess the price of an Old Master, or a Jeff Koons, at a glance. He could tell you how housing starts in Shanghai might affect the price of salt. Still, he never lost his taste for the philosophical. He could contemplate the meaning of space. On his fiftieth birthday his daughter gave him a silver cup engraved with one word: POET. He referred to it as his finest deal toy.

Anna always imagined her mother had left because being with a man like Noel was unbearable in a way. Everyone wanted a piece of him. Perhaps her mother never felt she'd been given her share. Perhaps her mother hadn't felt imprisoned at all but, rather, not quite imprisoned enough. Did the right interpretation of the past matter. Anna wasn't sure. She would spend at least part of the rest of her life trying to find pieces of that puzzle. By the time she was nearing thirty-three, and the arrival of her own puzzle, she had nothing but an outline of the story of her own life.

So much was missing. Speaking of the meaning of space.

Her mother's name was Lulu. Which had originally been Eleuthera.

Q.

A.

When people asked your father what he did for a living he would say, "I move things around," which we always found amusing. He always had an answer, didn't he. He was tough on us, and we deserved it, when you're new you're always a little stupid. He would look at you for a full minute, lean over your desk, and say, "You are in the business of realignment, that's all, you move things around. Don't get too noble about it." Any pretension about the profession sent him raging. I think that was one reason he chose me. We shared a simple philosophy. We believed that, like priests, we were called to this. And while we shared a strong cynicism about the work we knew there was no quitting it. You don't quit the Church. What we did—it's really just ordinary life, Anna, ordinary life sped up. Every interaction you have which clicks, you hold on to and build on. Every error, you either exploit or forgive. You work on your timing, you work on your ability to empathize. Noel told me timing plus empathy equals a successful recruitment, that timing plus empathy can even, occasionally, avert an attack. When I asked him to clarify what he meant by timing he said, "when to shut up, and when to talk." Timing simply meant knowing how to listen.

Realignment.

Lulu would call her daughter periodically and say things like, "Solving all the problems in Africa is not the same as solving all the problems in yourself," to which Anna would reply, "I'm not solving *all* the problems in Africa," even though she thought she kind of was, or that at least she was moving the ball. Like her father, Anna loved working on things that were foreign, or exotic, to others. She believed Noel had done that, too, that he had spent his days making complex mathematical decisions that resulted in wealth creation, though "realignment" was the word she heard him use most often when people asked what he did. "Realignment" doesn't mean anything does it, though it passes at a party, and then, as over time, friends believed they knew Noel and understood exactly what he did, they stopped asking. The more known you are the easier it is to hide, deflect. "Realignment" was Noel's defense against truly being known.

Anna loved her work for the foundation. She believed in Africa, and the idea that empathy and investment could create solutions to such diverse threats as AIDs, Ebola, the extinction of a species. Anna's belief in the work was a means to another end, a reason to stay late nights, an excuse to crowd out other experiences. Like, increasingly, love. Or commitment. At some point at some party when asked what she did Anna started simply saying, "realignment." She was doing exactly what her father had done, defending against being too known. Without even being aware of it, she was operating under a different kind of cover.

And Lulu observed all this from a distance and kept close watch on it. Lulu worried that her daughter was actually totally lost. She would listen to Anna talk about her life then say, "It sounds absolutely fascinating, but maybe you're just running away from all the baby carriages." And though Anna said nothing she was thinking that her mother was in no position to lecture anyone on anything. Especially running away.

Q.

A.

Anyone who has done a tour in a war zone has never done a real tour. The time from meeting someone to getting him or her to spy for you in a war zone could be ten minutes. In Beijing it could take ten years. Baghdad Station was the largest in the world then. Saigon was the largest station in the seventies. We're not a war organization, Anna, but when you're invited to a ball you put on a tux.

You're taught to ask an asset two questions when you meet her: *How much time do you have?* And *Did you get here safely?* A friend came back from Iraq when we were new though still cynical, and the polygrapher wanted to know if he'd asked the questions. He said, *I met my asset when he was running down the street screaming, "They're behind me!"* This is theory versus practice. "They're behind me" isn't espionage, it's anarchy. Often what we're engaging in is anarchy.

.   .   .

Q. A.

I volunteered to go to Iraq. I will never forget telling your father I wanted to leave where I was, telling him, "I want to be in the war." He laughed. "You're in the war, idiot." There was a map on the wall where we were and Noel stood up and pointed to the city I was working in then, in Asia. "Here," he said. "Here what," I said. I was cocky then. "It depends on your definition of the word *war*," he said. He moved his hand over the map, over Europe, over Asia, not stopping until his hand was hovering out over the Pacific Ocean. He looked right at me and repeated: "Here." And then I understood. "Choose your battle," he said.

And so I chose.

Risk.

When they were dating, the man who would become her husband told Anna his love of music came from fooling around in cars as a teenager. "You know, the radio," he said. Later he would tell her it was actually something else, a way out of his dyslexia, away from "the cage" of words. He would tell her that books always intimidated him while music never had. He would tell her how he felt complete confidence in his opinion of one thing—how something sounded. The first time he took her to see one of his artists, a female pop star who'd once played in bars but by then was selling out stadiums, they walked onstage before the show. He led her to the piano and she listened as he played. She realized he was also an artist, though he would shy away from that word. He played a simple song, one she recognized, and as it ended he hit one key over and over, *plink, plink, plink.*

"What is it?" she asked.

"A," he said. "The key of A." He told her what A major means, which celebrated songs had been written in that key. Then he leaned in and kept talking and kept leaning and talking until he was on her and around her. He led her away to some room in that stadium and when he said, "I am in love with you," it was not only the first time he had said it, it was also the moment she knew she could say it back, the ultimate risk.

She had never been the girl guys took backstage. She had never attracted someone so incandescent. She wasn't sure how where she came from had led her to him, to a world away from the one into which she'd been born. She was ready to travel. With him, she was ready. She felt complete confidence in her opinion of that.

Q.

A.

My grandparents went to exotic places. China, Russia. I remember my grandmother lining up little ivory elephants on the floor she'd bought in the markets in Asia. They were interested in the world, specifically in China and Russia, which is why those were the places I had wanted to go from a very early age. I wasn't interested in Rome.

A Chinese Embassy official pulled me aside after a press conference on the lawn of the White House once. I was young, only an intern. She asked me to go for coffee, which I did. She asked about my interest in China. And she offered me a gift: a white ivory elephant.

Over time you learn when someone's coming on to you for manners and when someone's coming on to you for need. You learn to deflect a sophisticated advance, or to flip a broad one. When someone wants something from you, you have power. Later, when

Q. A.

I would stay up nights in the safe house, I would ask myself what was so different about what I was doing from what that Chinese official had done. Absolutely nothing, is the answer. Nothing was different about what I would do and what was once done to me. Espionage is flirt and empathy before it's anything else.

HRH.

Rock stars. Arriving at the hotel for the honeymoon, Anna was thinking about rock stars. If she were a rock star, she thought, this was definitely the place she'd run away to, channeling lyric brilliance with room service and sunlight. It amused her to see her husband welcomed like a king at the desk. They knew him from past visits, trips he'd described to her as all parties and no sleep. He was HRH by transitive property here, via links to real rock stars, the ones he'd discovered and produced, here heralded for and there defended against a feral press, the ones he'd fawned over in greenrooms of late-night shows and cleaned up when being clean was required. The real rock stars, who channeled real brilliance in places like this one, on diets of foie gras and French cabernet. Arriving at the hotel for their honeymoon, her husband announced with apology that he had to go to Nice to see a band playing there that afternoon. She didn't want to go, and they didn't argue. When she asked the concierge for directions to the tennis court, he said, "What a perfect day for sports, love, swim, nap." And her king leaned, his hip against hers, and added, "Though not necessarily in that order."

Q.

A.

I had started taking classes on intelligence during undergrad and ended up in a seminar called The Intelligence Community. The stated goal of the class was to reinforce the necessity of intelligence, though I had the very clear if perhaps paranoid idea that the real goal of the class was to act as a sort of human resources outpost. One day the professor took me for a drink that became dinner. Four hours later he was telling me everything about clandestine operations. "*Clandestine* is something completely hidden from view," he told me, "as opposed to *covert,* which means something that appears as something else. Most people think they're the same thing." He asked me for my phone number, and the next morning I got a call from a woman who said, "I work at the recruitment center." The process had begun. A week later I was sitting in an unmarked office building in northern Virginia with fifteen other people. The meeting was framed as a chance for us to learn about the Agency but it was immediately obvious it was in fact a chance for the Agency to learn about us. Clandestine *and* covert, in other words. Everything we did was being observed.

Swim.

It's not quite sporting, is it. That's what Noel used to say about golf, mocking a thing that wasn't quite a game but rather posing as one, in his view. Noel never played golf but often used that line when the subject came up, as it seemed to increasingly as he aged. Anna had started using them, too. When the guy at the bar asked for olives, the bartender placed three olives in a small crystal dish. "Not quite sporting, is it," she'd said, and he had laughed. She was rarely laughing in those days.

After they'd returned from Switzerland, in February, Anna was sad and her husband was anxious, and the misalignment of their mourning moods caused a rift. His relationship with his own father was broken, so he'd started looking to Noel for things he'd never had, absorbing the whole Oedipal package in the process. One night that spring they were up late in bed. She was crying.

"I miss him, too," he said.

In the wake of the loss, she would see that the coolness she'd initially been drawn to in him was only a shell, easily cracked. They were entering a period of new depth, as happens after tragedy.

Swim.

.　.　.

"How about a swim," said the guy at the bar. He held out the last olive, an offering to accompany the invitation. She looked out the window down the gravel-lined lane that led from the hotel to the sea, lined by palm trees. She had nothing to do before dinner. Well, why not?

Q.

A.

The finest case officers are usually introverts. I knew some pretty fierce paramilitary officers who were extremely introverted, which you wouldn't expect if you track the clichés. *Introverted* doesn't mean you sit around and read and pray and don't watch basketball. It means you gather your energy in private. It means you don't need the party. One of my finest instructors was extremely introverted. It was one of her most powerful tools. When I asked her once if she was as shy as she seemed, she said she wasn't shy at all.

Her husband had been murdered in Lebanon. They had both worked at the station in Beirut. She was in her sixties when I met her. She delivered the speech and the lesson I would later deliver many times myself, the first speech you hear in the first class you take. The speech is designed to catch a fish, and someone always takes the bait. It goes something like: *Welcome. You are here today to learn what we do. We find vulnerabilities in people, and exploit them. Perhaps someone is poor. Perhaps someone has a gambling problem or a sick child or an outstanding debt. Everyone has vulnerabilities,* you say. *If exploited properly, every single person can be turned to work against their country in order to service their vulnerability.* Then you end with a variation on: *Welcome. Does everyone agree?* Inevitably someone shouts out, *Yes! Everyone is vulnerable!* That's your fish. Everyone does not have vulnerabilities, Anna. Vulnerability is a choice. And espionage is a crime. That's the lesson.

Each meeting in the early weeks takes place at a different location. You receive maps with no directions and have to find your way. The instructors talk to you about the art of manipulation and the necessity of discretion, that rare thing everyone admires but so few possess. Years later, I served with that instructor. She had worked with your father and knew him well. She was the one through whom I truly got to know him and later she provided the link when I needed his lifeline. She was pregnant at the time her husband died. She stayed on in Beirut and raised her daughter there. She said your parents came to see her, and the baby, on their honeymoon. She said they were the most beautiful couple she had ever seen. She said they were madly in love.

Trellis.

Anna thought about that swim as she sat at her desk, six weeks later, staring again at the first chapter, the first video, "Rooms," God, Heaven. Why had he sent her this? What did it mean.

> I believe there is a God, the little boy had said.
> And in His brain there are rooms, he had said.
> And there is a room where you can go and know if there is
>   a God or not, he had said.
> And also there is a room, where one dies.

He listed these things casually, without emotion, as one might list ingredients for the perfect chocolate cake. On describing each room he raised one tiny finger at a time—*for parents, for children, for friends.* It was clear to Anna that what he was saying was an answer to a question, that here was a child trying to make sense of things, as children do. He was trying to be heard. He was saying, *Of course there is someone who will protect me.* He was taking the biblical "in my Father's house are many mansions," and applying it to something he understood—a home. Anna Googled the biblical passage. *In my Father's house are many mansions, if it were not so, I would have told you. I go to prepare a place for you.* The little boy added the idea of a room where we go to know that God exists. A fine improvement, she thought. Though there was no mention of joy, no courtyard for her required space, no hibiscus or bougainvillea. There was no iron gate and no glass trellis, no view of the sea. Those had been her father's ideas. Noel, the poet.

She clicked back to the Menu page, the one with all those chapter titles, all innocuous words seemingly meaning nothing, "Rooms" for the one about Heaven's rooms, "Falcon" for the one with the falcon, "Christmas" for Christmas—you see the pattern. Anna looked at that list until she finally saw it, right in the center, staring, shouting, the one word that aligned with something relevant—to her. A word that echoed with what he had said the day they met. "Silencer."

"Silencer" opened with another home video, the little boy tying a bandanna around his brother's eyes, playfully, a child's game. The boy has on his most serious face as he instructs his brother to "tell me a secret." And then before the other boy can say anything, the video cuts out and goes to a blank black screen. Anna waited. She somehow knew something was coming. And then it did. Another video started. It was Noel.

He was seated at a table in an empty room with bright lights. In a high-backed chair, wires strapped to his chest and his wrists. It was a younger Noel, of maybe ten years ago, she could tell by the level of gray in his hair. He had taken his tie off and placed it on the table. When he looked up at the camera, it was as if he were looking right at her.

At that moment Anna wished she could crack open the laptop, climb inside, bring him back. She pressed pause. She wasn't ready for this, whatever *this* was, confession, indictment, reveal, apology.

. . .

"Of course I believe in you," Noel had said, standing behind her and holding her shoulders on the day before the wedding, Swiss sun shining through the icicled glass. She was looking in the full-length mirror at the chalet, wearing her wedding dress, after the final fitting. She was wondering what it would feel like to move from "fiancée" to "wife."

"Tell me again," she had said.

"I believe in you."

Q.

A.

Not once in the entire recruitment process did I ever see a piece of paper with the letters *CIA* on it nor did I ever hear anyone mention those letters nor did I ever set foot in Headquarters, at Langley. The letter of employment I would receive didn't say anything about the Agency, either. I showed it to my father and told him about the interviews and the buildings and the vulnerability speech. And my father said, *What makes you think these people are actually CIA?* He had a point.

I was told I had to undergo a background check, which included a polygraph. Ames passed the polygraph though Catholics, in particular, have a hard time with them. It's our guilt. I know a Catholic girl who responded, *I've killed Jesus,* in answer to the question, *Have you ever killed anyone?* The test administrator then said, emotionlessly, *And other than the son of God, have you killed anyone?* Belief systems can get in the way.

. . .

When the offer package arrived it had an eagle on the cover and a letter with a starting salary and date. It said to show up at Head-quarters, though it did not provide an address. Enclosed with the letter was a simple map, unmarked, of northern Virginia. Induc-tive learning, Department of Visual Effects. And the thing is, I had a moment of doubt. I had a moment of thinking, This is an absolutely insane thing to do with my life. Your father opened his speech in the China Ops course with, "Welcome to the asylum."

Provincial.

When Anna caught up to him, at the base of the path, he held his arms out wide, as if to say, *Look at me.* It wasn't a gesture of affection—it was self-deprecation; it was, *Look at me, in these silly red swim trunks. Look at me, so out of shape. Look at me, about to dive into the ocean with a woman I just met and don't know. Look at me, and trust.* She looked at him and thought, You're allowed to be happy, Anna.

When he'd proposed the swim she'd said it would be too cold.

"It's September," she'd said, though she'd packed her swimsuit.

"You only need to swim to where it's warm," he said.

"Ha, do you have a map?"

"It only gets warm once you've swum past the buoys."

He was her height, and looked maybe ten to fifteen years older, though his height and his looks weren't the first things Anna had tracked. The first thing she'd tracked was his comfort with quiet, like he felt no pressure to fill silence. It reminded her of Noel. Her father could sit for long periods of time without saying anything, a trait that drove Lulu into outer space with rage. Lulu felt his willed silences were selfish, that they were Noel's way of controlling situations by refusing to participate. "I have nothing to add," he would say, which wasn't plausible to anyone who knew him.

And of course what happens when one person says nothing is that another person talks to fill the silence, just as Anna had done at the bar. The guy she had only just met already knew some critical things about her while she knew absolutely nothing about him. She knew he was American. She knew he had been visiting friends in Paris and come south for the weekend. She assumed his work afforded him travel to places she'd never been—Jakarta, Beijing, Harare, Dubai. He told her he had lived in Hong Kong and that Hong Kong was provincial, that all the Americans there lived like kings. The casual pairing of "king" with "provincial" made her laugh.

"What's the definition of a provincial king," she asked him.

"Well, their definition involves lots of *golf*."

He said he gravitated to the Middle East because he found Europe boring. "Rome is provincial," he said. "Paris is provincial." Now he was teasing. He said the hardest part of living life in the places he did was that he spoke neither Arabic nor Chinese. Though that didn't turn out to be entirely true.

At the base of the path he held his arms out. And when she got to him they walked to rocky steps that led down to the ocean. You could dive right from the rocks, if you were brave enough. Anna looked out at the blue.

"Not provincial," she said, and dove in.

The water was cold. She wanted to see how far she could go underwater without needing to come up for air. She kept swimming until she could feel her lungs constrict, then pushed to the surface. She expected to turn and see him back at the shore. He hadn't struck her as someone who could keep up with her. Yet when she turned, he was right there, not even ten feet away. He'd been swimming alongside her the entire time.

"Jesus, you're quiet," she said.

"Practice."

Q.
A.

There was a girl in my class from California, all into the environment, who used to brag about how she took a bus to Langley, and I always felt like saying, *What kind of real spy takes the bus?* But you can't get into people's politics. You can't stand up and express your views, not at that level, not at the start. Your thoughts must be exclusively focused on only one thing: CIA *über alles.* Which is to say, not the ozone layer. Pick your battles.

CIA 101 is a weeklong introduction to the Agency, where they read you in. On the first day you get your top-secret clearances. One, called Keyhole, is named for satellites, the view from space. You're given a pseudonym, and the protocols around using the pseudo are explained, like how on email the last names of pseudos are always shown in caps so you can easily know when you're communicating with someone under cover. Tony Q. HAWK, say, or Barack H. OBAMA. In that class there were future officers, analysts, lawyers. It's important to befriend the lawyers; you will need them later. The various directorates come and give lectures. Years ago this was all done at the Farm but at some point someone realized not everyone needs the Farm. Lawyers don't need to know how to jump out of planes. Case officers don't need to know, either.

On breaks I would wander around the in-house museum. My favorite piece in the collection is a large wooden plaque that was given to the U.S. ambassador in Moscow by a group of Russian schoolchildren. He hung it right over his desk at the embassy where it stayed for several years until someone suggested it be examined. It contained a sophisticated listening device. The Russians had kept transcripts of everything said in that office. After that, no one said very much in embassy offices.

I was assigned to an office in China Operations. China and Russia are the most restricted parts of the Agency because of the counter-espionage risk. Most doors at Langley don't require locks or codes, but to enter the China division I had to ring a buzzer and wait. Someone eventually opened the door and said, *Yes?* So I told them, *Yes, hello, I work here, may I please come in,* and they shut the door. When the door reopened it was Noel. I was told he had once been a branch chief within China Ops, an outlier, a cowboy. He had long before stopped working there but came around. I wouldn't learn how to be a case officer at the Farm. I would learn from him.

Lobster.

Have you ever told a lie? That was what Anna asked him.

In response he had laughed and said, *I've literally lied to every single person I've ever met.*

They were swimming slowly back to shore. She was thinking about acts of omission. She was thinking about how she would describe her afternoon, if asked about it. Perhaps it was simply a swim.

As they walked up the hill to the hotel he told her a story.

"Bill Donovan founded the Office of Strategic Services during World War Two. He was so excited about the development of the silencer he took a twenty-two into the Oval Office."

"A gun?"

"And Roosevelt was there alone, on the phone. He didn't look up when Donovan entered. He didn't look up when Donovan said his name. So Donovan said his name again, and when the president didn't look up a second time, Donovan fired the gun."

"At Roosevelt?"

"At the wall. He only wanted Roosevelt's attention."

"I should try that sometime," Anna said, thinking about levels of distraction, about attention she had needed at different times.

"Well, don't try with a silencer."

"What happened to the wall?"

"Eventually, it was repaired."

Eventually everything is repaired.

They said goodbye, Anna thanked him for the olives and the stories and the swim, and he thanked her for the company. She went up to her room and slipped out of her suit, then crawled into bed for a nap. When her husband woke her, he did so gently. It was already dark, and they spent some time together before dinner as she thought about the hole in the Oval Office and silencers, and he thought about how blessed he was to have this beautiful girl. He was committed to helping her find peace.

They went for dinner late. Her husband had insisted on Champagne so she'd had just a sip. Champagne reminded her of her mother, who stocked the icebox with six-packs of miniature Perrier-Jouëts. She drank it on ice, claiming it sped the metabolism.

After oysters Anna excused herself to wash her hands but walked past the WC out into the night. The sky was filled with stars. And there he was, smoking.

"Hey, Roosevelt," he said. And then, "I'm trying to get your attention." The sly tone was ironic, and disarming.

"I liked that story," she said. She watched him take his cigarette and flick it out over the garden, sending an arc of orange light into the sky.

"I should go," she said, after a few minutes, after a few things had been said. She held out her hand, as we all do when saying goodbye, and he took it in both of his, briefly, before letting go.

Her husband had started on the lobsters without her. A side plate was already piled with cracked shells. Lemons had been squeezed and crushed into a bowl. As she sat down he looked up, barely registering she'd been gone. He was cradling his phone on his shoulder, though on seeing her he put it down on the table, leaving the call running on mute. He held his hands out, as if to welcome her, as if to indicate he wanted her right then. She looked at his hands and thought about the hands that had just held on to hers.

She leaned in for a kiss. She looked at the shells.

"I am sorry, I couldn't wait," he said, like a child.

She forgave him. She always forgave him.

Q.

A.

On my first trip, to Africa, I was accompanied by an older female ops officer. I was shy and wouldn't have started a conversation, but as we took off she turned to me and started talking. She had a whole theory about espionage and why people go into it. Her theory was that only broken people want to spend their lives avoiding deep emotional commitments with loved ones while establishing deep emotional commitments with people they will eventually betray.

She told me there's a fine line between flirting and not flirting, and that minding the line was critical to career advancement. She said in her view men are simple and that you need to know only two things about a man to understand him: who he's in love with and what his Achilles' heel is, what he needs and what he fears. I asked her what happens when what you need and what you fear are the same thing. Well, then you're fucked, she said.

. . .

Eventually she told me, in a very calm and even voice, that her husband was leaving her. She said it as if she were reading the weather report. And then, maybe in exchange for my empathy, she proceeded to deliver a detailed character analysis of every single officer, every chief, current and former, in China Ops. I learned that your father recruited his most gifted asset through a friend whose daughter was living with her at Harvard. Her code name was a digraph, FX, tacked onto the word *veritas,* the Harvard motto, Latin for "truth." She was, at that time, a kind of chimera in China Ops; everyone knew of her existence but there were layers of coded, classified architecture around her, who she really was, where she lived. All I knew at the time was that Beijing listened to Veritas and Langley listened to Beijing.

One night we were eating at this gorgeous café on the water, in an East African country, waiting. Suddenly people started getting up from tables and walking quickly away from the shore, as if taking part in a choreographed exodus. I hadn't heard a bomb go off. I had no idea what was happening. In excellent, accentless French, my colleague asked the waitress, who said, casually, "They know to be home before dark." We paid the bill and got up and started moving fast, too. We reached our hotel minutes before they shut the doors. One week later, that officer would resign after being placed under investigation for an interrogation she'd overseen. That trip taught me about the difference between emotional and literal chaos. Something can look quite still and be in a state of total chaos, as she was. Something can look chaotic when in fact it is absolutely controlled, like the running in the streets.

Christo.

They'd flown home early from France. He had no choice, he said, and she understood, it was work and a good wife doesn't argue with work. At home, she tried telling herself it was fall, time for new things, time to let go of last winter and of the girl she had been since then, time to participate in the ritual of starting over, as one does in September. She told herself all of this. Then ruthlessly rejected her own advice.

And also there is a room.
    The boy in the video who describes the rooms in Heaven looked basically the same age that Anna had been when Lulu left. A child of six is capable of expansive thoughts.
    And also there is a room.

At first, when Lulu left, Noel told people she'd gone to Europe, and Anna remembered him telling people how she had moved from Paris to Berlin. Anna had still never been to Berlin, but she'd always wanted to go ever since reading about how Christo wrapped the Reichstag. She remembered there had been a debate in the Bundestag surrounding whether or not an artist should be allowed to do this, and was it art. Should an artist be allowed to wrap Germany's iconic Parliament building in aluminum and ropes? And if it was art, what was it trying to say. Was it saying something about hiding, or revealing, or about the political position of the empire, the newly unified nation. Was it a lark. "The children will love it," one of the politicians said, during the debate. She was reading the article only because any reference to Berlin reminded her of her mother.

Later, seeing the extraordinary silvery image on the front of *The New York Times,* she thought that the building looked like a ship. Maybe it wasn't a statement on politics at all but rather a statement on seeing, on how we cease to see things we are accustomed to. For every German who spent decades walking daily by the Reichstag, the Reichstag, in effect, had disappeared. Perhaps it was a statement on how things we see all the time often cease to be seen.

She had called her father to discuss this. When she called him at the office he always played cool, as if he were having yet another dull day, though later she often would learn that some crisis had been rising at the time, the price of gold imploding, an IPO gone awry.

"Things don't cease to be seen if they matter," he had told her. "Art that makes the Reichstag invisible poses the question of whether the Reichstag matters. It's a statement on paying attention. We pay attention to the things we care about," he said. "Paying attention is the cardinal sign of love."

Her father had always insisted on skiing off-piste, that was part of the lure of those mountains. He'd always preferred to ski alone, claiming it was his time to think. So the fact that he'd gone alone with his skins and hiked to an altitude prohibitive to someone half his age wouldn't otherwise have drawn attention. Snow had been predicted, though. When it snows hard, one can get disoriented.

Speaking of patterns of seeing.

It hadn't been her idea to marry in the mountains. It wouldn't have been her preference to plan a memorial at the moment most girls plan a pregnancy. One day, there were two glimmering rings and a party planned in Manhattan. One day, her father held her shoulders and professed his belief, knelt to check the length of her hem. That was Noel, focused on precision and detail in moments of emotion. The seamstress, at the fitting, told Noel she'd never fitted a bride with her father before, to which he'd replied, "I'm her something old." One day, there was only expectation.

Later, there was a reckoning, not with what would be but with what would not. There would be no walk down any aisle, no something old or new or blue, no bouquet. There would be only Anna in jeans, and the local minister who married them in front of the fire. When the fire wouldn't light, Anna knelt down and started ripping pages from the local Alpine paper to place under the wood. Eventually her husband gently pulled her to her feet.

"Hey," he said.

"I don't want to wear the dress," she said.

"Of course you don't."

Later, in bed, he said, "No one will ever love you like he did." He was trying to be kind, to acknowledge the new absence in their lives. She hadn't heard kindness, though; she had heard a confession. And unconsciously she would try, for a time, to see that he lived up to the crime.

October wouldn't be any easier. Especially after the arrival of the video, which she initially considered a kind of post-scriptural gift from the guy at the bar, on the swim, and later interpreted as a sign from her father for her to empathize and understand, and ultimately understood as a kind of map and lesson. Anna didn't want her last image of Noel to be in that room, though, or even on that mountain. She liked to think about him in Heaven, returning to poetry, flirting with angels.

In the video, after he identifies the photograph of the Chinese girl, after he looks at the camera and says, "Veritas," Noel is asked about espionage's limits, or perhaps about his own limits, depending on your view of the question, the questioner.

Noel is looking at the camera, breathing very slowly.

I don't understand the question.

Is anyone off-limits for exploitation. In your opinion.

Exploitation?

Recruitment.

In my opinion?

Yes.

Noel thought about this for a moment. And then he looks up and right into the camera.

Angels.

Angels?

Angels are off-limits.

Anna wondered whether patterns of seeing existed in Heaven. Could one, even in Paradise, cease to see a thing. She decided yes, even an angel might cease to be seen.

Q.
A.

Fireside chat isn't only a phrase we know from FDR, it's also a spy thing. A fireside chat occurs when a senior case officer reads an asset's file and arranges to have the asset flown somewhere in order to "chat" with them. It's usually somewhere quite beautiful, like Bali. The chat takes place after the asset has been producing and is well known. The senior officer flies to Bali and they will sit for several hours, sometimes days, talking. During the *interrogation*, which is in fact the right word, the officer hits on issues that bothered him while reading the asset's file. They call these "fireside chats" because they're meant not to sound hostile. They're meant to sound cozy. Bali's not a black site.

Occasionally polygraphers are present at the chats, which is not cozy. You were just swimming the Madura Strait; now here comes the Spanish Inquisition. Assets rarely think about polygraphs so most are surprised when they have to submit to one. You, of course, are always thinking about them. Technology frightens people. You know that, despite the fact that you might have distributed millions of dollars over the last eighteen months, there will be that one cab ride that comes up in the poly and they will nail you if you misreport its fare.

The true mission of the Office of Security is to answer one question: *Are you a spy?* But there should be a level of respect. The person being polygraphed should be allowed his dignity. A polygraph is the opposite of dignity. The beginning of a very long poly is *Did you sleep with her?*

When Ames was being hunted and when Hanssen was being hunted, the Office of Security was focused on a third man. That third man underwent months of polygraphs, and through it all, he maintained his innocence. He was cleared only after both Ames and Hanssen were proven guilty. You see, the real mission is to make you crack. Making an asset who is acting as a double agent crack is one thing; making a loyal servant crack is another. This is what they did to your father, Anna. Though they argue they were simply trying to get at the truth.

Truth is a spectrum. Understanding this is a matter of emotional intelligence, which can slip in the presence of stress. Or in the presence of overconfidence. If you think you possess the magic lasso of truth, you might err on the side of overconfidence, you might lose that most essential human instinct, a will to empathize. Absent empathy, there is no understanding, no intimacy. Absent empathy, are you even a man?

Bali's not a black site.

Or is it?

Intimacy.

What is intimacy?

Anna had always been looking to replicate that original deep connection, looking to get back to that kitchen, those eggshells, her father's rolled-up shirtsleeves. The rolling up of those sleeves was a way of committing.

In the months after Noel died she would try to cook, only to find herself unable to finish even the simplest thing. She would market, and prepare. She would read recipes. Then she would order pizza. Her husband, accustomed to having his meals ready on arrival home, found this unsettling.

"Maybe we should get some help," he said one night.

"What kind of help?" She was picturing a hospital room.

"Like a chef?" When he wasn't sure how she would react, he often framed ideas as questions.

"The use of the word *chef* is what's wrong with the world," she responded, thinking how at one time people simply called them cooks, but now everyone who reached a certain level of life had to have a chef, had to have things prepared, had no mess to make, let alone to clean up. Her husband had increasingly taken to car services then, flying first-class, and other forms of economic insulation and grandeur. She felt it was an assault on her values, all this ostentation. He felt it was simple practicality.

"I want to make it easier," he told her.

"If you hire me a chef I am leaving," she said, pouting, and they both laughed and let it go and it was pizza and rage for six months before she went to him and said, "Maybe one night a week we could get some help."

"Why don't I just take you out once a week?" And they started this tradition and it lasted three weeks. He was busy. She didn't care. He was scared. And she was numb.

Numb and lucky, is what everyone around them thought. She had married a wunderkind, after all, a prodigy who had won his first Grammy at twenty-six, who seemed to have started out of the gate to adulthood minting money through art. How glamorous they were, at that gate. And Anna initially absorbed the admiration of her husband's peers, who found her Ford work inspiring, if foreign, the idea someone might work hard for no financial return, engage in things like curing diseases, or famine. She found his set cool, if exhausting. How many times can you eat dinner at eleven? How many times can you wait backstage and express awe, and gratitude. Sex had been there once but had evaporated early, leaving only the experience of success in its wake. The experience of success can be visceral but it is also cold.

Their lives lacked intimacy.

Neither one of them wanted to blame the avalanche; that would feel at once too easy and too real.

They had paired as their peers had, on education and rule, though he was more editorial in his choice; he knew how to spot a unicorn and trap her. He liked that she'd grown up on Fifth Avenue. She liked that he'd dropped out of Brown to produce a record with friends. When one of those friends founded a label, he'd gone along for the ride, and would ask her to come along, too, when they met. "I'm going to be in *Rolling Stone*," he told her casually, on their first date, at the River Café in Brooklyn. When he asked her to marry him only weeks later, she said yes and he said, "Really?" The speed of the proposal was interpreted by those who knew him as characteristic, his lack of patience, how when he wanted, he wanted. When he wanted, he took. Though the speed of the proposal was in fact about his insecurity. He was desperate not to lose her. First date to proposal was less than a year, though it would be a while before they got around to a wedding.

The engagement party, though they called it that, actually wasn't one, as it took place the fall following the wedding. They had five hundred, mainly his list, most of whom seemed to be publicists or other players from the concentric circles that formed around artists. He found a space on Wall Street or, more precisely, above Wall Street, on the highest floor in the tallest building. It looked out over everything, including the reflecting pools.

"I have vertigo," Anna said when she walked into the room, saw the view.

"Oh, baby, if you fall, just use your wings."

Around midnight a few of them snuck off and boarded a sailboat owned by a record company. There was a captain, and a crew, things to eat passed on trays, probably molly in the bathroom, though she never saw it. They cruised the harbor and anchored near the Statue of Liberty. Anna was thinking, Wow, though no one said "Wow" out loud. One rarely commented on the spectacular in this set.

This set, his set. They had a kind of earned entitlement, a sense they were where they were because they were gifted. This philosophy was foreign to her and, as foreign things often are, initially seductive, before reason or instinct sets in, before we return to ourselves. She lay down on the deck and looked up at the stars. She was wondering whether all the exceptional moments in her life would now come through him, whether that was in fact what she had said yes to, the exceptional, an exceptional life.

He came over to lie down beside her. She pointed to the Statue of Liberty and said, almost defiantly, "Wow." He rolled to face her and said, "You're better than wow."

Intimacy is the ability to understand what someone is trying to tell you. Intimacy is listening. It was in that period, when she was looking for that deep connection, for something to make her feel again, that the package arrived in the mail.

Donovan used the silencer because it was a cool new toy. Donovan also understood that when you're going to do something spectacular, like place a bullet in the Oval Office wall, you need protection.

Q.

A.

When I started you'd have two phones on your desk, black for outside calls and green for "internals." The evolution of encryption is cyclical, at some point someone always says, This process isn't working for me, I need to make this process less transparent. At some point someone always says, Get me a better phone. Only a better phone is an illusion, you can't trust phones. The only thing you can trust, aside from talking face-to-face, is a letter with one author and one recipient. A letter has a level of control.

An Aardwolf is a letter from the chief to the director or even the president, and it's one person's thoughts and impressions, which is to say it's not necessarily intelligence. Unlike reports its tone is intimate, candid. Forty-Three famously had his Aardwolfs delivered in person. Kennan's "Sources of Soviet Conduct" was a kind of State Department Aardwolf. I am sure you know it, your father's favorite. Kennan was writing from Moscow in 1946 and essentially saying, *Hey, Mr. President, you think you know the Soviets but you don't. Let me tell you who they are. Let me tell you because I am here, I understand, I see clearly.* You can't see clearly unless you're there. I think your father loved Kennan because he also felt

misunderstood. He never wrote a "Sources of Chinese Conduct."
I think he would have liked to. Sometimes pure intelligence can't
capture the nuances of a situation, especially in a crisis.

Your father wrote me letters he called his "Aardwolfs from the Station of One," by which he meant the philosophical station he then
manned from retirement, halfway around the world. When Indonesia was blowing up they sent me to Jakarta; I ate ice cream at the
Hilton while the Marriott was bombed. I took that job after your
father wrote a letter about Indonesia's importance, and after he sent
me a handwritten note of two words, "Take it."

Crisis.

Her mother. Her mother had done everything right, so why not throw a wrench in that record and do something spectacularly wrong.

When she was a little child, Anna's understanding of her mother was based on this idea of a record begging to be broken. Her mother's choice, she told herself, was a question of patterns, of expectations, of record. Records of Everything Right are not only unsustainable, they're exhausting. Girls who do everything right occasionally need to smash a phone into a wall.

This was how Anna processed the idea that a parent could ever leave a child. And as with all rationalizations, this one worked until it didn't, until Anna grew up and needed something more specific, like an answer, or an apology. Because letters don't quite cut it, do they, even ones as beautifully written and carefully conceived as the ones Lulu had sent through the years. Lulu poured herself into pages of descriptions of a place or an idea or an emotion, as soldiers on front lines once did for their lovers back home. It wasn't quite the right form for a parent to take with a child, especially a parent who had abdicated the throne.

The day his wife left, Noel had blown into the kitchen and, with an air of disbelief, said, "Your mother's gone." The kitchen was off the foyer lined with gray de Gournay paper. An armada of magnolia leaves always exploded from a center, circular table.

Noel knelt down to his daughter's height and repeated himself.

"Mommy's gone."

"What?" was all Anna said.

"Mommy's gone away." And then he added, "And I will never leave you."

He didn't cry so she didn't either; little girls cue off their dads. Eventually Anna could barely experience anything without checking Noel's views on it, affording his views veto power over her own. The night Lulu left, Noel let his daughter eat dinner on a tray in his bed watching cartoons. She remembered the tray was made of red lacquer and that she ate Lucky Charms with half-and-half. She didn't know he had placed her in his bedroom so she wouldn't hear him crying in the library.

It wasn't in Noel's nature to show emotions, not that Anna would have seen them if it had been. He threw himself into the act of replacing the absent parent, as if it had been his fault his wife left, though everyone knew it wasn't. Every teacher conference, every tennis lesson, he was there. Once people had early-era cell phones, Noel was the first to adhere to strict protocols of when it was appropriate to use one, and when not. When: at work. Not: at home. When: in emergencies. Not: in crises.

"What's the difference between an emergency and a crisis?" Anna asked.

"Length of duration." He always had a view.

Anna became a proxy for her mother, growing up fast enough to play the role of partner for him in ways. It was an arrangement that worked for both of them. By her twenties she was so used to assuming the role of date, or hostess, she no longer thought about where she ended and where what her mother had once been began. There would never be a stepmother, but there were lots of "girls." Noel named them numerically—*One* and *Two* and *Three*—et cetera. As in, "Opera with Two tonight." Or, "The French Open with Five." It was his way of keeping it casual, preserving distance. Or perhaps it was his way of protecting Anna, providing the illusion that he was always open to her mother coming home.

The girls came and went, most electing to leave before being demoted by Noel from "true potential" to *"femme du jour."* There was a brilliant Swiss economist, who arrived with tiny Toblerones from duty-free. There was a British MP who brought teddy bears from Hamleys. A Russian ballerina who gave Anna her first set of toe shoes, which she never wore. The ballerina hung around. She didn't mind being "available."

Once, in that era, her father had taken her to a state dinner at the White House in honor of the president of China. Anna asked if China had evolved from an enemy into a friend.

"Countries are people, too," was Noel's answer.

All she remembered about that night was that her father spoke perfect Chinese and seemed to know a lot of people, and that the first lady wore red. Anna eventually concluded the difference between an emergency and a crisis is that an emergency means life-or-death while a crisis means *I need someone to listen to what I am going through.* By thirty-five, she hadn't yet suffered an emergency, but she was living more or less in a permanent state of crisis.

Q.

A.

I finally arrived in a station where I would stay for a while. I was increasingly confident which is of course when God throws you that ball. God manifests in many ways in the intelligence world, usually to remind you that however brilliant you think you are, there is always someone who knows more. Whenever you think you've arrived on the inside, it's revealed there's another level of classification off-limits to your level, another nesting doll inside the one you inhabit and have come to call home.

I was a consular officer. That was my cover job. I was actively and every day and all day looking to recruit an asset, to accomplish what we'd been taught was the goal, which is completing the agent-recruitment cycle. They call it a cycle and draw it in a circle even though it's a timeline. *S* for *spot, A* for *assess, D* for *develop,* which is courtship, a little seduction, and lots of promises. During *D* the asset's issued a code name. Then *R* is for *recruit,* when you finally pop the question. And you never ask that question unless you know the answer with absolute certainty. Once she says yes, you're in business. There are no more trips to Rio. You're married, you're running the source.

T is for *terminate.*

If at any point you're asked if you're CIA, you're trained to turn your answer into a question. You're trained to say, "Why, what do *you* think about CIA?" I've looked into the eyes of many men and women and said I have absolutely nothing to do with the Central Intelligence Agency. I've developed sources in strip bars and in Starbucks. I've pretended to know Bill Gates and Bono. I've even claimed to be descended from the finest horse-breeding family in America.

I believe in ends and means, Anna. I believe there are some things that simply can never be said.

Hard Targets

What can and can't be said. Anna had ideas about this, some learned, some developed. Her father raised her to say less as a rule and, as life got complex, she found this rule helpful across categories. Certain things simply couldn't be said.

She decided it couldn't be said that she had met a man on her honeymoon who knew her name and who knew her father and who told her he would send her something in the mail, something related to her father.

"It's not a bomb, is it?" she had asked, sort of teasing, sort of not.

"Actually, it kind of is," was his answer. "Though it won't hurt you."

It couldn't be said that in addition to the video there was a note and a series of photographs held together with a silver money clip engraved with the Chinese character *chenmo*—"silence." The photographs had place-names written across them in red ink: MANILA, JAKARTA, BEIJING. They were photographs of her father as a young man. One showed him wearing formal Asian dress with a pretty girl on each arm. The girls were wearing light-blue silk flowered dresses and their faces were purposefully blurred. Anna had seen faces purposefully blurred like that in history books, or sometimes in tabloids. It's a protective measure. Written across that photograph right below the word NANJING was written HARD TARGETS, a joke. The girls' dresses reminded Anna of new curtains she'd put in their apartment downtown. "My something blue," she'd said aloud to herself, as she'd installed them the morning of the engagement party.

Do you have a daughter?

Noel plays with the tie on the table.

Yes.
What's her name.
Anna.

Noel looks into the camera.

Grace.
Grace?
It means grace.

The note was written on a card with her father's initials at the top in gray Roman font. Two words were written in his hand: *Take it.*

Take what?

Q.

A.

The Farm is about buying into an idea. It's about participating in a tradition that started with recruitments at Yale in the forties, with Des FitzGerald and Tracy Barnes. It came down by way of those Cuban beaches, to Tora Bora, to today. As you go through all of the absurd exercises, through car pickups, brush passes, dead drops, you think about the people who preceded you. As you learn about verbal paroles and visual recognition signals, you have a sense that understanding these things will be important to ensuring national security. What else can you tell yourself? You have to make it have meaning.

It's called the Farm because where it is looks like farmland. It's beautiful. It's the preeminent espionage training ground in the world. And it's in rural Virginia, and no, they don't make maps of it to sell in any gift shop. There is no gift shop. There is no Farm. Most people know exactly where it is and what it's called but it's still technically classified. It's a massive, sprawling complex, a military base, basically. When you walk around you might see people jumping out of planes. It takes thirty minutes to drive across the campus, though no one calls it a campus, and it's actually prime real estate. The only thing that shatters the idyll are gunshots going off. When on occasion we have visitors flown in, the pilots black out the windows. As they descend they will sort of loop around so the passengers won't know where they are, in theory. I mean, at least they make the effort. The illusion of location classification in the age of Google Maps is just that, an illusion. We hold on to certain illusions because they matter. Though I wouldn't try to storm the Farm gates.

I started as a clandestine service trainee on a Sunday. I remember because I'd called home and my mother was telling me about the sermon planned for that day in our church. She said it would be about Moses and the thou-shalt-nots. I think she was only saying that to taunt me. She had become increasingly concerned with what she felt was a sort of moral relativism in my line of work. She'd skipped right over glamour to the ethics of the thing. I always admired her for that. Most people stop at glamour, in my experience. Most people mistake this vast bureaucracy for a Maserati fueled with intrigue and sex.

None of the doors there have locks. Everything you do is observed all the time, by everyone; you are ranked, though the rankings are secret. The Farm becomes home, becomes life, for six to nine months, sometimes more. When the fire marshal spoke to us at orientation he said, "I have no idea what you guys are doing here, I'm not cleared for that, all I know is that I have personally installed smoke detectors in each of your rooms and I want you to know, *there is no camera in those smoke alarms,* so please don't rip them out." He'd spent a lot of time replacing ripped-out smoke alarms.

What they do to you over those months in this elegant laboratory is a test of trust. If you lie in bed long enough looking at one of those alarms, you begin to doubt. You begin to doubt yourself. Even if you know you are being observed, over time human nature—or let's call it desire—prevails. Over time, people are going to do whatever they are going to do to survive.

You are introduced on your very first day to a mythical place, a country that does not exist but within which you will be operating now, as if you were newly stationed in Austria, or Chile. You're given policy briefings on illusory policies. Your instructors impersonate diplomats who don't really exist but who serve on behalf of this foreign place. And while there are very real police stationed right outside the Farm gates who carry very real guns, once inside you find another level of law enforcement, cars marked with symbols of the fictional place. You are told to respect them as if they were real.

So in this one place, which technically does not exist, you find another place, which literally does not exist. The former has no map though the latter does. It takes attention to remember where the real ends and the illusion begins. Later, you apply this same skill to yourself. Once you start deploying, you require an ability to know where you end and where you begin, which nesting doll is at your center. You won't want to lose track of the belief that the last and central nesting doll is you, the real you, your soul. Until you have to.

The Farm is about buying into the idea that not one, but *all* of those nesting dolls are you. The ability to inhabit all of them without doubt is essential to survival.

Baby.

When you don't really have a mother you are likely to be ambivalent about becoming one. Anna was. Her mother had left when she was so little, but she had stayed in touch. There were always cards for special days and lavish Christmas gifts, always unexpected visits at the most inconvenient times. Her mother operated on the assumption she was wanted and welcome, despite her poor choices. Lulu lived adamantly opposed to the idea that her choices left wreckage in their wake. In the weeks preceding Anna's wedding she began calling her daughter daily, beating the drum about a baby. Already. And ironically.

"I'll forgive you for not including me in your wedding if you forgive me for telling you you're on the edge of your fertility," she told her daughter, who was then barely thirty.

"Edge?" Anna asked, wondering whether the fertility graph looks like a line or a bell curve, deciding it looks like a cliff. "And we're not having a wedding, we're having a minister and Daddy and that's it," Anna answered.

"Is your fiancé too fancy to include me?"

"He's not fancy at all, he's busy. It's logistics. We will be there because we love it there and it's Valentine's Day and we can ski." There, Switzerland.

"Well, you'll need a dress," Lulu said.

"Yes."

"And you should think about a baby."

"I will add that to the list, thank you."

Anna hadn't given having children much thought. For the first time in her life she felt a sense of calm, of order. She felt she had someone who would take care of her. In those days, she wanted what he wanted. She would have a baby if he wanted one and she might not need to if he didn't. It was classic premarital logic, which is to say not logic at all. It was a certain phase of love.

"Do we want a baby?" He laughed when she asked him. "Stand up. Put your arm out." And she did.

"I am going to press your arm down," he said. "Like this. If you want a baby you will resist against my pressure, if you want a baby you won't let me push your arm down to your side."

"What is this game," she said, and held her arm out. He never ceased to surprise her.

"Trust me," he said.

Though as he started to press down, she drew her arm back.

"I don't want to play," she told him.

"It's not a game."

He explained he had learned this from his thesis adviser at Brown. He described going to meet his adviser fall of junior year, terrified to say he was considering dropping out. "I didn't know what I wanted, I wasn't sure. I wanted his blessing or I wanted him to tell me to go. He told me to hold out my arm and think about what I wanted. He said, 'Do you want to stay in school?' When he pressed down on my arm, I didn't resist. Then he made me put my arm out again and said, 'Do you want to leave and make music?' and he pressed down and I resisted."

"I don't understand," Anna said.

"The body knows."

"Knows what?"

"Sometimes we don't want to put words around a thing. Even if we know what we want."

He lifted up her shirt and knelt down and kissed her on the navel. "The body knows, baby," he said.

想—the Chinese character for "want" literally means "I am thinking," though depending on the context, it can mean "I want," too. When Anna's boyfriend, who would soon be her husband and who would rapidly take their lives in an entirely unexpected direction said, "The body knows," her response was, "Well, this body is keeping that knowledge a secret."

Q.

A.

There were six students in the unit I was part of at the Farm. One was a Delta Force officer who'd recently completed an inpatient program at Walter Reed. His family was invited to join him in the final week for a series of psychiatric sessions. He'd told the doctor he didn't need the sessions, that he was fine and performing well past par, that he didn't believe in psychiatry, that post-traumatic stress was a liberal conceit. The doctor asked if he believed in science. And then he held up a scan and said, "You have nineteen lesions on your brain. You need help." Sometimes we can't feel or see the injuries we've sustained. Sometimes there are no scars because sometimes the body lies.

To commit espionage, you need a place to do it. You learn how to select a place, how to travel to it undetected, then disappear. And while you don't want to meet an asset in Times Square, you don't necessarily want to meet them in the desert, either. Choosing places is an art. By the end of my time at the Farm I could map the cities of Richmond and Williamsburg in my sleep.

Sometimes you meet an asset you've never seen before. You know the person you are meeting is the person you are meant to meet by using a classic trick called a "verbal parole." It's a pre-agreed-upon exchange, something you say plus something the asset replies. A parole stays with you for the course of a career and for the course of the life of an asset.

You can lose track of an asset, of course, if something goes wrong. A war starts, a coup. Your father famously once reopened a relationship after a decade using an old parole. He was witty with his, of course; he always keyed them to history, things like, *How is the winter in Moscow? Ask Napoleon.* The most important parole I would ever use was, *Are you waiting for Sweet Virginia? Yes, my name is Ron Wood.*

Lions.

Anna thought the video would tell her why Noel went up the mountain that day, and who those men were leaving the chalet as she returned. She thought it would say something about the reason and the cause, something about Noel placing his downhill ski at such an angle that he set the shelf of snow in motion, it was a choice, it was a plan, at least that would make it clear. At least, she could picture that. And forgive. He had never said goodbye. When she arrived home that day she had passed the men on their way out, they were wearing suits and shoes not suited for snow. She'd gone straight to the porch where she'd found the remains of the lunch, cheese and bread and fruit, a bottle of red wine uncorked but untouched. Anna remembered looking at the plates and telling herself she would clean it up later, that first she had to clean up *herself.* She had gone back inside. She had taken a shower. Her husband was away purchasing the rings, though they had chosen them together. He would arrive home that night and she would cook supper; Noel would serve as sous-chef for the fondue. The correct temperature for oil to boil cheese versus meat was on her mind as she stood under the water and washed the blood off her face from the slip she'd had at the base, a tiny cut on her jawline, not serious. Everything was laid out on her bed for the following day, her dress, shoes, white ribbons to wrap around the bouquet. She put her hair in a towel and, wearing a robe and boots, she cleaned the porch, washed the dishes, checked her phone. There was a text from her mother sending love. Anna wrote back that she loved her, too. She called the minister and they talked about her wish for simplicity in the service. He asked if she wanted anything else read aloud, perhaps a poem, which led to talking about poetry. She told him she'd tried to find something about joy but had failed, how all her favorite poets wrote mainly about despair. "Joy is less interesting," said the minister, who was Irish, and understood poets, which made her laugh. She dried her hair, put on jeans, and opened a book. She hadn't once wondered where Noel was, she'd assumed he had gone into town to buy bread or out for a walk. Her mind wasn't moving to places of worry that day it was moving to calm. Around four o'clock she fell asleep, snow was falling. When the avalanche started less than half an hour later, it woke her, it sounded like the mountain breaking open. At the start, an avalanche sounds like a low roar, like thunder. Or like lions.

Q.

A.

What is intelligence? Intelligence is information leaders need to keep us safe. Though all information isn't necessarily intelligence. Intelligence has to be new. Time and relevance are critical. If an MI6 archive newly reveals that Churchill's sister served in Paris under Vichy, that's intelligence. Saying Putin has offensive cyber-weapons, that's not. Before and after meetings with your asset, you talk to the reports officer and she gives guidance as to what qualifies as intelligence. Intelligence isn't found via a search engine. And it's rarely found via a polygraph. The day they traveled to see your father, they weren't looking for intelligence, Anna, they were looking for confirmation. Those men who came up from Geneva weren't there to absolve him, which was what he was told. They were there to indict him, and to have him indict me. They were three hammers in search of a nail.

Little Dipper, North Star.

Her husband would hate it if he ever thought he was hurting her. On their "honeymoon," he wasn't tracking Anna's drift. Which is why he wasn't worried when she walked out of the restaurant that night. He saw her go. He may have even seen her talking to another man. But he didn't know what they were talking about, and when she returned he didn't inquire. She was his now, that was that, proposal, ring, boom, done. His confidence in the institution of marriage was sort of interesting, given his distrust of institutions generally. At least, then.

What else had he told her that night. A story about a polygraph. The whole idea of the polygraph struck Anna as very strange, like a form of torture.

"It is a little like torture," he had said, laughing. "Though one doesn't make jokes about torture." The story was about someone who was so upset by the question he was asked that he had simply stood up, torn off the wires, and walked out.

"Can you really tear the wires off?" she'd asked, thinking that sounded so radical, thinking it was something she would never do.

"Yes."

"Have you done that?"

"No."

"Tearing wires off sounds painful," she said.

They were looking at the stars while her husband sat inside on one of his myriad mobile devices, changing the world. They looked at the stars and he said, "No one ever said to Van Gogh, 'Paint a starry night again, man.'"

"What?"

"Joni Mitchell."

"Joni Mitchell?"

"That's what she told her audience once."

"I like it."

"Any artist can tire, even of their masterpieces."

"Yes. Or simply tire of performing on demand."

He took a step toward her and didn't say anything. At that moment, she had elected to believe it was absolute coincidence they were meeting again, now.

"When you lose someone you love, you only want to be around the people who loved him, too," Anna said. She had one hand on her stomach.

"Boy or girl?"

"I don't know."

"He loved you."

"Yes, I know," she said.

"Do you know why he tore off the wires and walked out?"

She could see the Little Dipper, the North Star. She could hear Noel saying, *Make a wish, kid.* "Yes," she said. "He was tired of performing, too."

Q.

A.

At the Agency everyone thinks they're better than everyone else. It's human nature. The analysts think they're the brightest, and the operatives think they are. The Special Activities guys think they are, as they have a combat background. East Asia looks down on Latin America, and in China Ops we thought Latin America was absurd. Though perhaps they are simply relaxed. When my colleagues in Santiago launched surveillance routes they would stop and get haircuts on the way. In Hong Kong, you took hours, sometimes days, to plan each route, each site, each parole. You had to be meticulous. Of course the Russia House guys think they're the brightest, the tip of the American intelligence spear. This is the essential quality of the place. Everyone's at the tip in his own mind, it depends on your description of the shape of the spear.

Where you land is determined through a series of conversations and trades in a room you never see. After you graduate, the division heads sit around a table and talk and barter. It's a draft.

Everyone wants the best picks. And people gravitate to environments that match their temperament. Some guys want to take siestas and drink sangria. Some guys want to date Thai girls. I had studied China. I spoke Chinese. Arriving with my profile and not wanting China Ops might make someone think I wasn't playing straight. It might place me right back in the laps of those magicians with their coins.

I fell in love with China before I went to work against her. Your father understood this choice, he had lived the arc of that contradiction, too. He had grown up looking to China as an example, and he admired the Chinese people's aesthetic. He admired their sense of history. He was meticulous, as you know. He was private. He was at peace with a little moral relativism if the end justified the means. He could sit through a meeting without saying a thing, then, at the end, deliver the most important analysis of the situation. Or in stations, the most important intelligence. He was forgiven his certain arrogance. I was told that in an early polygraph he responded to the question, "Are you faithful to your wife?" with the question, "Why, are we in kindergarten?" He wore that side of himself rarely though, he was never sharp, always looking for ways to elevate others, ways out of taking credit. He knew credit came with prominence and with prominence came risk.

His China Ops talk opened with him pointing out that when you arrive in certain divisions, like Africa or Europe, they congratulate you. When you arrive in China Ops there are no congratulations. A door opens and you're asked when your last poly was. And at that everyone laughed, we had all experienced that, that's how traditions evolve. You experience something, it shocks you, then you replicate the experience for the next guy in line. Your father's China Ops talk ended with him saying, *If you're not comfortable with hypocrisy you can leave right now.*

He knew suspicion is contraindicated with confidence, that a lack of trust explodes trust, self-fulfills our worst prophecies. He would say, *We must trust one another or die.* Or, *Ten guilty go free lest one innocent hang, yes.* He would say, *This is America, come on. Loyalty.* Your father understood the shape of the spear, Anna. Glamour comes from being at the tip, but power comes from elsewhere.

Dare.

"Truth that" had become code between them. Her husband might say it to deflate a crisis or to place Anna at ease. He would say it walking into parties that he knew made her nervous, he would whisper it into her ear before the start of the season of endless awards shows; there was always just one more and she was shy on the press lines. He would say it before they dove into icy East End pools or before taking tequila shots at the Carlyle bar. "Truth that" meant "It's true" but also "I'm here." Increasingly it meant "You're not alone."

It was a reference to the one time they'd actually played Truth or Dare, on their third date. They were at a friend's house uptown and after dinner someone suggested it, almost ironically, though then they all threw themselves into the game. Dare was the prefer-ence. These were her friends, which is to say not a daring group rather one prone to privacy and discretion. Dares for them felt illicit. His friends would all have opted for Truth, they had enough real risk in their lives and their art. Things escalated and started to get racy which made the wives nervous. On his turn Anna's hus-band stood up, raised his hand, and said defiantly—he was the first one—"Truth." His answer to the question, *Are you in love,* was to walk over to Anna and kiss her, look her right in the eyes, and say,

"Truth that." And then he said, Let's go home, which he knew was what she really wanted. Later, lying in bed, he'd taken her hand and placed it over his heart.

"Truth this," he said.

The day they'd arrived home from the Cap, he had called her from the office.

"Truth or dare."

"Truth," she said, always her preference.

"I sold the baby."

The company, the baby, it was done.

"It's over," he said, and she didn't ask the number, she could guess by the sound of his voice. Before she could tease with a question, like, "Does it mean freedom?" he added, "Let's run away together."

Let's run away together is what he would have said first had she said, "Dare."

Q.

A.

Ask someone on the outside of East Asia, but within the director-ate, and they will say that East Asia has a terrible reputation. It's like the Ching dynasty, they'll say. It's a bowl of snakes. They will say East Asia officers treat their chief like an emperor. I would say in East Asia you simply go through the chain. I have a friend in Africa division who calls his chief on his cell phone. He goes to his chief's house for breakfast, and for Christmas dinner. He brings girlfriends to his chief and asks for his blessing. Chief East Asia will never meet my girlfriends. I don't have his number. And I highly doubt he celebrates Christmas.

In East Asia every door is always closed and our cubicle walls extend to the ceiling. Africa division looks like the *New York Times* newsroom, there is freedom and there is chaos, like Africa. If an East Asia guy walked into that division he would panic, all that sharing of information. And in Latin America they sit around like, *Do we really think the Guatemalans have scored a coup and recruited an Agency guy? No, let's go drinking.* It can take a long time to ensure your place in China Ops, though once on the inside, I was imme-diately embraced. I had the right teacher.

Nobel.

Happiness was the topic at the table that night, a black-tie dinner at a midtown club. Anna grew up on these dinners and in these clubs, though she was invited now not because of her father but because of her husband, who had developed an unexpected and ardent interest in politics. The baby sale had awakened something in him, perhaps. It had certainly placed him in a position to act on an awakening. The morning after the deal was done, after all the contracts had been signed and all the lawyers placated, he'd turned to her in bed and said, "God, what now," and she realized he didn't know the answer. With the sale came, too, an end to the acceptable period of mourning, and Anna was increasingly expected to show up, emotionally. Her husband needed her now, who could blame him. He had gotten what he wanted and was spinning in the wake of new options.

Political dinners were rarely festive, at least according to her definition, but Anna went along as her husband had started donating to campaigns, and donations lead to dinners. This all might have been admirable but for the fact that Anna was sure he didn't know whether he was a Democrat or a Republican. He'd never had allegiance to ideas, only to people. He tended to vote when inspired by a candidate's charm. Noel's view had been that politicians' personalities were beside the point. Her husband's view was, "What else is there?"

Anna found his new political passion both alarming and amusing, depending on the moment, on whether she felt it was evidence of crisis or of a kind of renewal. They were both growing and changing, he as a result of the sale and new prominence, she as a result of loss. And while they never discussed it, they each silently hoped their changes would run on parallel tracks and align. In a nod to that hope, they'd each decided that a baby, a real one, would be the shared goal. Parenthood's a fine proxy in the absence of true alignment.

The dinner was to celebrate a former cabinet member and her memoir. Her speech was dry and Anna's dinner partners weren't listening. They leaned behind her and made jokes about the upcoming election, how the state had no serious candidate standing in the party of their choice. They had little interest in Anna. Across the table she could see her husband's rapt attention to the speech. She thought about the Statue of Liberty, that crowd versus this one. She thought about the skill her husband had in moving through crowds, shedding shells or perhaps growing new ones as required. It never seemed to strike him as contradictory or cynical to spend one night with pop stars and another with politicians, while it made her feel a sense of longing for home and place, for her people, though his people were her people now, too. She wondered whether she had reached her place in life and would now rest in it, the role of good daughter gracefully having evolved into the role of good wife. She had sorted her father's affairs. She had calmed her mother. She had chosen a husband who would love her without fail. She looked across the table at her husband and wondered what he was thinking.

"One of my professors won the Nobel for studying happiness," the man on her right, who had gone to Princeton, said.

"I read that study, about the set points, how we each have a happiness set point," said the man on her left.

"I think countries have happiness set points, too."

"Well Italy's is high, China's is low."

"France is *very* low."

"All Europe is low, I'm afraid. Except Italy."

"Happiness is anticipation," said the man on her right. "Happiness is having something to look forward to, though you might just call that ignorance, or illusion—hope." Anna looked at her husband and mouthed the words *Help me.*

"Respectfully, I think that's a lie," her husband said, speaking up across the table. It was the first thing he had said all night. "Happiness isn't anticipation. Happiness isn't Christmas Eve. What we want is not what comes before a thing. We may not even want the thing itself. We want what comes after. Peace, accomplishment, the chaos of new challenges. Those challenges are essential to understanding ourselves. Happiness isn't anticipation at all. It's the presence of new challenges that lead to self-knowledge." He looked at Anna, and winked, and mouthed, *I love you.*

In that moment Anna realized she was the one spinning in place. He was moving forward. She watched him as he became the center of the table and of the evening, as he moved first to speak to the cabinet secretary, and then as her dinner partners moved to speak to him. She envied him. She wanted to find her way out of her point on that graph. Why couldn't she just stand up, tear off her wires, and walk out?

Q.
A.

What is an absence of trust?

Trust, Lesson One.

At the Farm they used roadblocks as teaching aids to help you learn how to conceal things if you're stopped and searched. When you encounter a roadblock, it's all very serious and true to life, the fake police flash their lights, they remove you from your car, they cuff you. They have drug dogs, weapons dogs, explosives dogs. Sometimes they plant baking powder on you then ask why a U.S. diplomat is carrying cocaine.

I was never sure if they were testing our trust of one another or our trust of ourselves. What we trusted about one another was that we were all participating in this illusion with the understanding that there are limits to illusions, the understanding that no one was going to get hurt. What we trusted about ourselves was that if we felt the game wasn't being played fairly, we would have the courage to say so.

One night a few of us came upon a roadblock. They stopped

our cars and had fifteen of us lined up in cuffs along the road. They told us to kneel. Suddenly, a guy stood up, broke away from the line, and started running. Everyone was wondering, *Wait, should I be running, too?* The mock police released a real dog that chased him.

No one said anything. We watched him go down in the grass, and no one stood up and said, *Hey, this has gone too far.* We were lined up facing the field and one by one they placed us in police cars and drove us to the fake station and herded us into the fake jail. Later, we were told it was all a show. Later, we were told how that student was selected and run through rehearsals. We were told about the vest he wore to protect himself from the dog's teeth.

Trust, Lesson Two.

A New York City cop shoots an unarmed boy. At the crime scene, the officers who arrive to investigate find two untraceable pistols under the body. The body is lying facedown and when the officers turn it over, they find one pistol by the boy's chest and another by his pelvis. And they immediately understand. The first pistol is a play to save the life of the cop who has shot him. The second is insurance on the salvation. The pistols have been placed by other cops. In the station we used to say, "Place a pistol." It meant, Secure the plan. It meant, Tie up the loose ends, watch your back, protect your team.

The thing is, Anna, a police officer is empowered, you're the law, the thin blue line. Case officers are not empowered, you're not the law, you're running away from the law, you're ether. You do your work and evaporate. An unarmed boy shot by a cop constitutes a crisis. When a case officer creates a crisis his colleagues rarely slip a pistol under the corpse.

An absence of trust is a fox in the henhouse, Anna. At a certain point you ask yourself whether it is more important to protect the truth or to protect the culture of trust. At a certain point you ask yourself what happens when the fox is let loose.

Cake.

"Trust me," he said, placing his hands over her eyes. She had miscarried, and in the car home from the hospital he told the driver to keep going, and they'd driven all the way past Amagansett, almost to Montauk, a new February frost coating the trees. "Trust me." And then he was walking behind her, his chest knocking her back, as he guided her to the little kitchen of the cottage they'd rented by the beach. "Look," he said. And then he stopped and opened his hands to let her see and she saw that the room was dark but for the cake, its lit candles creating a picture of risk, and invitation. What was the risk. What was the invitation. He slipped his hands down to her hips and then gently but forcefully turned her to face him. He moved his hands up to her eyes, just in time to catch the tears. "Make a wish," he said. His nose was on hers and she could feel his eyelashes, almost an Eskimo kiss. "We will get through this," is what he told her. Because that was the risk, wasn't it, that this time they wouldn't get through it, that one day some fresh crisis would finally break them, belie the myth of the depth of their bond. And the invitation was for forgiveness, not of him but of the gods, of whomever it was who had delivered to them this day, this loss. Anna would accept the invitation. She would be at peace with the fact that risk is simply what we live with in love. After she blew out the candles he led her upstairs and ran her a bath. He sat by her as she bathed and then he took her to bed. In the morning when she said, right into his ear, "Hey, this is my wish," he believed her. He found relief in making their emotional chaos Cartesian. She found relief in convincing him he could heal it all.

Q.

A.

A shiny thing is a thing everyone wants, that one brilliant recruit. There was a time when I did a lot of chasing shiny things. A lot of spotting, assessing, developing, endlessly filing reports and trace requests, dreaming up cool crypts and taking assets on outings to please and seduce them. Eventually I was given the chance to run one and only one asset. She had access to the head of Chinese intelligence. She had access because he was her father. A very shiny thing.

The rumor was that she'd been given to me as a test, that the chief was thinking to deputize me if it went well. That rumor held, and became accepted history, but it wasn't true. The truth was your father had described me to her and she had chosen me. We were the same age. We had a similar temperament. We were both religious and had both run away from where we came from, from who we had once been. Your father had known her for a long time, and when she was ready to work for us, she went to him. He told her about me, then introduced us off-line, and he was likely the one who told the chief I was the perfect one to run her. I hadn't spotted her, or assessed her. She had spotted and assessed me, in a way. And she would develop me, too, until it was time for her termination.

Key.

One palm open, one palm closed. The open palm was empty.

"I'll give you another chance," her husband said.

"How generous." She had guessed the right hand, she always guessed the right hand first. This was a game they played—candy, theater tickets, folded love notes.

He came to her and sat by her and slowly, dramatically, opened his left palm. And there it was, a tiny gold key.

"What do you think?" he asked her.

He had bought a new home, the home they had looked at and loved but that she had said they could not afford, the one in a new neighborhood that suited his new identity, uptown, with rooms for children they didn't yet have and a dining room for dinner parties they had never given. It had started with his saying one night that they needed a "real place," maybe one where he didn't line skateboards up inside the door, where books didn't spill from shelves onto the floor in unruly piles. She was adamant against this idea of needing anything but it was increasingly hard to brook his enthusiasms. It was his money now. It would be his choice. And he had been so exceptional around her losses, why shouldn't she be enthusiastic around his gains? This wasn't war.

"What do you think?" he said again, leaning in to kiss her

behind the ears. And Anna looked at the key and she could see the small office her father had once had, with the water cooler, and she could also see the other office, the great glass box, and she could see Noel rolling up his sleeves and strapping on his skins and she could see the men in their red jackets with the wide white crosses.

"I love you," she said, what else could she say.

Q.

A.

Once the word was out about her, congratulatory cables came in from every office that held a stake in her case, which was every single office. In those moments you tell yourself you've advanced the interests of national security, despite the paperwork and the anomie, despite the kneeling at night watching a dog tackle your friend. Your father sent a note, too, though his were always handwritten. "Follow the truth," it said. Later, once she was classified as Restricted Handling, there were no more notes, and then eventually it was clear to me that I would have to turn her over. Occasionally a turnover is a relief, assets can be exhausting, she certainly was. Though more often it's a shock. You're putting your baby up for adoption. You made her. She's yours. And the letting go can prove excruciating. Though I don't mean the letting go of the child, I mean the letting go of control. In order for everyone to feel at peace, to let go, to begin again, a turnover has to be perfect. And there is no such thing as a perfect turnover, Anna.

Falcon.

In the bedroom of the new home there was a canopy bed and twin nesting tables that had belonged to her grandmother. There was a long mirror on the wall with a chinoiserie frame her husband had brought back from a business trip. He liked standing in front of it while holding her, "Come on, show off a little," he would tease, which she never would.

This was where they would make a new life.

This was where she would solve the riddle.

Here, Anna had an office, or what her husband had called an office, a little alcove off a library. She'd never had her own space before; she was used to working at the kitchen table. He had given her a beautiful antique wooden desk, though there was nothing on it now except her laptop. When he was out she opened it and played the video again.

In its second-to-last chapter, the one after "Silencer," the one called "Falcon," there is a desert, and nothing but dunes. It looks like the Middle East, or Africa. It looks hot, a place best left to kings and falcons. Then a young man runs into the frame. Anna can see he is chasing something, slipping in the sand in pursuit.

When the camera closes in on him he is wearing a T-shirt, and he is laughing. When Anna looks at him now she immediately sees his ten-year-old self. What preceded the dunes was a series of thirty or more scenes, starting with the monologue about God and Heaven's rooms and followed by snatches of a life—kitchen suppers, Christmas mornings, birthdays, the presentation of a puppy, the presentation of a diploma. Which is to say, everything in every other life, the rituals we all endure and celebrate. Everything in every other life until those dunes, which were exotic, which seemed like an outlier.

Though there is another way of seeing it. A falcon in a desert is not an outlier, after all, it's an experience. A falcon in the desert is not a clue. A child with a vision of Heaven that aligns with the vision her father described to her, that's an outlier, that's a clue. And seeing it that way, Anna realized that what she was watching was not the story of where one boy ended up but rather a story of where he started out. The video was a way to let her see someone first and foremost as that little boy, a way to humanize him, to help her understand what came after, the things he did and saw, the choices he made. The video was a request to be seen not as he was at the bar or on the beach or that night outside the restaurant, but as he once was, before he grew up into the role Noel prepared him for. Anna envied that little boy. She didn't envy the simplicity of snowball fights or the splendor of a falcon. She envied his belief. Everything about him led back to his view of those rooms, the belief that they existed. Or maybe he simply sent the video so she could see her father answer questions that would come up.

Did the officer overseeing Veritas ever commit espionage against the United States of America?
Not to my knowledge.

Noel looks very, very tired.

May I have some water, please?
Did you train an officer in how to commit espionage against
the United States of America?
May I have some water, please.
Are you now or have you ever committed espionage against the
United States of America?
No.

The time stamp on the video read 4.56, four hours, fifty-six minutes. Under that was one word, TRIPOLI.

The video was the case officer's way of telling Anna his story, and allowing Noel to tell his, too, before someone else arrived with a different version.

It was his way of cultivating her trust, though she didn't know that, or experience it that way, at the time.

Q.

A.

She was an outlier, also, a cowboy in her way. After she soared through Harvard and LSE she'd returned to China and needed money, or so she claimed. She was in active rebellion against her rich family, one known for breeding rebels. By the time we met, she had reconciled with her father. That peace was critical to national security. A false peace, entirely illusory and built upon lies, received in the station with popped corks and steaks, a peace that would change my life, and hers. A peace brokered by Noel.

She was the perfect asset, entirely unremarkable. The fact that she looked like a child was part of her power, though she was approaching forty when we met. That agelessness aligned with an ability to fold herself into fables about who she was and where she came from.

Your father didn't develop her in the traditional sense, Anna, but you see he took the long view. He had met her when she was seventeen, in Adams House, on Bow Street in Cambridge. He would predict, then orchestrate, the next three decades of her life. He would select her crypt—Veritas.

I have often wondered how much of my life he also orchestrated.

Noel could quote the Four Noble Truths and within an hour refer to church as "the magic show." Somehow, he was at once fascinated by belief and devoutly atheist. Eventually I understood that enlightenment for him was being at peace with internal conflict.

If you're not comfortable with hypocrisy, you can leave the room right now.

Drones.

Do things happen for a reason or don't they. One must choose what to believe. Anna believed reason takes its place behind emotion. A girl meets a boy in an atrium entirely by accident, falls in love, and later marries him. Reason or emotion—or both. A girl meets a man for a swim on her honeymoon, hears his story, and elects to help. Reason, emotion, call it a draw. A video of your dead father arrives in the mail, you are moved by it, you make choices. Emotion. What is our responsibility to things that happen to us. What is our responsibility to reason.

A part of Anna wanted to throw the video out, make it disappear. Only we can't throw things out anymore, can we. Everything is virtual now, forever present. She could delete it off her home screen, or whatever it was called, but it wasn't *going* anywhere. And in truth, part of her wanted to throw it out but another part of her wanted to post it on YouTube, an invitation to the man who'd sent it to come back into her life and finish what he'd started. A part of her wanted to break the shell of her situation, see what she could make from what was inside.

And anyhow she didn't know how to post something on YouTube. She didn't know how to post something, period. She hadn't yet tested out social media; it all seemed equally rabid and casual, this obsession with documenting every breath, lick, bruise. Who cares about what you did last night. Anna felt it was tawdry, a view that amused her husband, who, despite three phones and myriad email accounts, had hired a social-media adviser to tweet and post and like things in his name all day long.

"Whither privacy," she said, observing him at his desk late one night, scrolling Instagram while listening to a conference call on mute. The call was about the upcoming elections.

"What's *whither*," he said, popping an earpiece out of one ear. He was teasing her.

"It's all just too much," she said, nodding at the screens laid out in a line like children: iPad, iPod, some other thing she didn't even recognize, a tiny silver globe emanating blue light. She pointed at it. "What's that, a drone?"

"It's a speaker," he said, laughing. He could play all these toys like a piano. He was cooking up something new, though she didn't know what. His contract required he stay on as CEO for a year, though it was clear he was now running two things—the company and the launch of a new iteration of himself. She worried he wasn't getting enough rest, though rest had never been his thing.

"Come to bed," she said.

When he finally came into the bedroom, she was almost asleep, willing dreams of peaceful things, clouds and gardens, per her doctor's orders. The chief of obstetrics had said stress works against the body's ability to make babies. He'd said her stress levels were too high. He'd encouraged acupuncture and meditation, though she'd failed to find time for either. Thinking happy thoughts before bed she could do. Clouds and gardens were simpler than needles in the spine. And so she was starting to think about summer planting on the island, maybe peonies, when her husband entered the bedroom. He was holding her laptop and it was open. The video of Noel was playing. He tapped the volume key.

—ever commit espionage against the United States of America?
No.

He pressed pause.
"What's this," he said, calmly, "a drone?"
Do things happen for a reason? Anna believed they did.

Q.

A.

In order to interrogate someone effectively, you have to have patience. You need the ability to listen for long periods of time when nothing is being said, knowing eventually something will out. You try to frame interrogations as conversations even as everyone in the room knows what's what. One thing that comes out of the Farm experience is a weird ease with being observed. Eventually, you've spent so much time with these people you really don't care who sees what anymore. And that ease translates into a certain confidence, which is the inverse of anxiety. You simply can't get worked up about surveillance, surveillance is part of life, that's how it is. Gentlemen don't read other gentlemen's mail, they used to say. Well, not until gentlemen are up against an enemy who flicks her wrist and shuts the lights off at the Super Bowl.

There's an inflection point in training after which no one rips out the smoke alarms. The inflection point is when you make the choice: The absence of privacy is a price you're willing to pay to do the work you need to do. Which, of course, when you're starting out, you describe as saving the free world. You look at that smoke alarm and think, *Saving the free world, motherfucker.*

Q. A.

What you learn at the Farm is basically how to decouple patience and anxiety, how to listen in complex situations and remain calm. Look an asset in the eyes and deny you're CIA, and feel calm. Listen while a prisoner tells you when the bomb will go off, or where the enriched uranium is, and feel calm. Threaten someone's life, and mean it, and feel calm.

Secret.

"Tell me a secret," he'd said on their swim that day at the Cap. And so Anna had asked him what the definition of a secret was. They were far out, farther than she would have gone alone. The weather was turning and the water was freezing. And though she was a fine swimmer, she'd never loved the open ocean.

She had simply followed him. She wanted to seem brave though she didn't know why, she didn't know this person, why should she care what he thought? He had led her so far that when she looked back, the palm trees were visible only as tiny dots. They were treading water. She was tired.

"A secret is something only two people know, and then mutually elect to keep private," he said.

"That sounds so serious," she said.

"Well, it is."

"And what if a third person enters the picture?" she asked.

"Well, then it's no longer a secret. Then it becomes intelligence." He was laughing, and it was affecting his tread.

Anna took a deep breath and let herself go under for a moment. In school she could swim the length of an Olympic pool without coming up for air. She'd been arrogant about her ability until she met a big-wave surfer. Some surfers can hold their breath for four minutes, the time it takes waves to complete a set.

She couldn't see the bottom clearly but she could make out shapes. She tried to dive farther down but could feel her lungs under pressure. When she came back up he was still treading water.

"I have a secret," she said, eventually, blinking water out of her eyes. She wasn't looking at him. She was looking at the palm trees. She was thinking about her husband.

"I have one, too," he said. And then, "You first."

"I'm pregnant."

And she looked at him, and for the first time she saw he was disarmed.

Q.

A.

Toward the end of your time in training, patience wanes and your last day is absolutely barbaric. You're shepherded into this pink auditorium and told to wait quietly while in an adjacent room instructors make their choices. You can sit there for an entire day. Eventually, an instructor enters the auditorium. She will go to certain people and tap them on the shoulder. The tap means you're done, you're out. At Yale they have a tapping tradition also associated with spies. Being tapped means you've been chosen to be in one of the secret societies. It means welcome, *Welcome to Skull and Bones, James Madison the Sixth.* After everyone tapped has left, the instructors say, Congratulations. That's it. It's over.

The director flew down for graduation in a Black Hawk helicopter. As we were all undercover, when he calls you up onstage he uses only your first name. You are presented with a simple framed certificate. You walk across the stage and there is a woman holding out her hand to take the certificate back. She places it in a box and you will never see it again. You held it in your hand for less than a minute. That was your moment of recognition. When the woman takes the certificate you are reminded that from here on out you will no longer be yourself.

This erasure of self is seductive to a certain temperament. There is a kind of person who experiences the drop of a certificate into that black box as fascinating. It's a complex trick, to tell yourself a black box leads to a calm, normal life. Though the other way to see it is that they're upending ideas about graduating. This isn't Goldman Sachs. This is the Central Intelligence Agency. You don't need a certificate.

After the ceremony, I walked outside. Your father was there, at the edge of the woods. I hadn't seen him at the ceremony. I hadn't seen him in some time. He didn't put his hand out, he simply nodded at me and said, *"Tempus fugit, sumus hic."* Time flies, we're here. Or said another way, There is no turning back now. There is only moving forward.

Supermodels.

He never knew.

Anna never told her husband about the first time. He had been so busy with the sale. With all they had on that fall, there hadn't been time for clouds and gardens or acupuncture. She'd lost him at eleven weeks, barely a month after the end of the honeymoon. She'd told herself a baby lost at eleven weeks was not a tragedy to define her but rather an experience to be managed privately. Still, she took it out on herself, retreated into herself. By Halloween, she felt better. They'd been invited out and her husband had dressed as Henry VIII, early Henry, slim Henry. He'd suggested she could be Jane Seymour.

"She's the sexy one, the one he loved," he put it.

"Yes, the one who died," Anna said.

"Oh, but he loved her so much before all that," he said, adjusting his paper crown. "Let's pretend she was the first wife, then he never would have gotten fat and they would have lived happily ever after."

Happiness. His happiness set point was stratospheric. It would almost make him freakish if it didn't make him so winning. That set point had seduced the artists he'd signed and likely also seduced the buyers for the company, a consortium including an Asian financier planning expansion into China. Jake didn't go little, when he went, Henry VIII, of course. Excess absolutely exhilarated him.

Jane Seymour wasn't for sale, though, so Anna went with her default option, a black cat, which required only a mask. The party was held in an old fire station two sugar heirs had blown open and renovated into a sleek steel loft. There was barely any furniture, or perhaps it had been removed for the occasion. Everything was beige. Even the circular staircase was beige stone and tile with a polished brass banister. "It's from France and it's fake and I love it," said the wife, of a statue in the front hall. She had a Ph.D. from Penn and was dressed as a Robert Palmer girl.

Anna's husband was very protective of her that night. She suspected he knew something. She had recently pulled away in bed, not that that meant miscarriage, but still it was a signal. Even on their hardest days they always found each other physically. After France she'd seen the doctor for the first time and he'd told her not to rush back to sex, and she'd ignored him. When she returned a second time she told the doctor she was fine, that she had moved on, she didn't mention the bleeding and the fact that she still felt pain.

Her husband kept telling everyone at the party that night about Henry VIII's favorite cat, implying that that was Anna's real costume. "They had a mouse keeper just to fatten the mice for her," he told their host, who was dressed as Richie from *The Royal Tenenbaums,* in tennis whites and aviators.

One of the artists from his label arrived, she'd been central to the sale. She was there at his request having promised to sing a little, "bring the sparkle," as he liked to say. The artist reminded Anna of an alien, all smooth and silent. An alien, adept at climbing up on things, pianos, other women's husbands' laps. She wasn't wearing a costume and Anna envied the confidence it took to not wear a costume to a costume party. When she arrived she announced loudly, "Christ, guys, I'm playing for the president!"

"The American president?" said Anna's husband.

"And I am not going to fit into anything," she said, prompting the question and inspiring the reply, "Yes, fourteen weeks," which resulted in a loud round of congratulations. "I think a white beaded tent will fit," she went on, everyone chiming in about how well she looked.

Anna suddenly felt like she couldn't breathe.

Everything around her suddenly felt fleeting and light—proximity to pop stars, imported French stone stairs, name-dropping the leader of the free world. Like cotton candy, certain experiences evaporate the minute you taste them. She took off her mask. She asked her husband to take her home. In the cab he held on to her.

"I promise you will have one, too, soon," he said. He'd almost read her mind. But he couldn't read her future.

At home, she felt ill again.

The body knows. The body never lies.

At Thanksgiving, he flew to Hong Kong for work. At Christmas, it was Shanghai. He always offered to take her but Anna always declined. She responded to the next set of pregnancy tests with grace, and wore her rage in private. A baby will come, is what she told herself. And a baby will change things. Her husband's success had recently shifted the math of which one of them needed the other more. A baby would come and a baby would need her. A baby would have no one else.

After the second miscarriage, only weeks before Valentine's Day and before her birthday, weeks before the anniversary of the avalanche, Anna announced that she didn't want to work anymore. She had finally told him about the baby, and when she did, she had also told him about what had happened in the fall.

"Maybe you felt if you told me it would make it real," he said gently.

"Yes, maybe."

"I think working reduces stress," he said. "I think you should keep working."

He was balancing worry with charm.

"Yes, stress," she said.

He didn't mean to say something to speed the shifting math. She had been filling a glass bowl with chocolate hearts and she suddenly stopped.

"I just want it to end," she said.

The next week she stopped working. She started acupuncture. She forgot, for a while, about the swim and the video and even, at times and in flashes, she forgot about her father, or perhaps she was simply getting better at willing away the facts.

That period in their lives was bookended by two parties, the firehouse on Halloween after the first miscarriage, and a restaurant downtown in early March, after the second. The restaurant had high ceilings, and though there was still snow on the streets, the owners had opened their doors to let tables spill onto the sidewalk. Anna and her husband sat at a banquette underneath a Peter Beard photograph of some supermodels and an elephant.

At the bar a group of schoolgirls drank vodka shots. Anna looked at them and thought about that age, before we make the choices that define us.

Her husband had insisted Anna sit next to him. They were right at the center of the banquette.

"What if I need to escape," she said.

"Just slip under the table. Let's slip under now, just for practice." He was holding her hand, and he wouldn't let it go all night, not even to eat. Anna didn't know what to talk about at dinner parties now that she wasn't working and couldn't yet talk about children's schools. As the volume of the table rose, she was quietly gauging how hard slipping under the table might be. Someone was talking about digital music meaning new markets.

"Once we launch in China I can pivot," her husband said. Which caught her attention.

"Pivot what," she said, eyeing the girls at the bar.

"Pivot to something new," he said. "A quiet life. Gardens."

Anna closed her eyes. He was teasing, of course, his life would never be quiet. He had one speed, and it was increasing. Could she keep up? What if she simply didn't want it all anymore. Does not wanting what you have qualify as a secret? If it does, would this one also vanish before she could share?

two

Q.

A.

The night before I left for Beijing my parents gave me a ship's nautical compass with a tiger's-eye stone set in the center. "So you can always find your way home," my mother said. She wasn't referring to Asia; of course I could find my way home from there, and my mother wasn't so silly as to see Asia as exotic. She was referring to something else. What she meant was that the compass would remind me that sometimes we lose ourselves. Sometimes we need a way to return to who we are, if the center slips. The center is what can get lost.

As I spent hours on that boring visa work, I was newly living in a state of constant heightened awareness. Before deploying, there were no worries about hostile control, no worries about safety, about whether my accent was passable, about whether I could recall on demand where I had been at this hour on that day and with whom, what I had paid at that bar or what color lipstick the waitress was wearing. I had entered a new phase, the one where you can't forget anymore. You can't misplace. Life is no longer casual.

One day I was on my hands and knees in my office looking for a button that had popped off my blazer. Your father walked in without knocking. He was wearing a traditional Chinese jacket with an American shirt and tie on underneath. I would soon start seeing him regularly, even as he wasn't "in" anymore. He knew my chief, who had been his protégé. He knew his way around the station. He looked at my desk and saw the gift. "A moral compass!" he said, like a child spying candy. "Exactly what I've been looking for."

Pills.

A marriage can last a long time in a state of gray. A state of emotional limbo. Anna knew her parents had lived that limbo, that her father had been increasingly absent in the early years of the union. And whenever she forgot this fact, her mother would remind her until over time she no longer wanted to argue with Lulu over the definition of *absent,* over who had been more or less present. Everyone had seemed to admire her parents' bond until the bond was broken. In that generation people talked about what happened when a marriage split up but in private, the topic still retained the gloss of taboo. Anna was never sent to specialists to deconstruct her response. The response of a child was beside the point.

A marriage is a walled fortress, rarely accessible to even the most sophisticated external observers. That fortress is one of marriage's gifts, and Anna experienced this gift acutely in that year of chaos, the one her husband would later refer to as their *annus weird-abilis.* When this or that friend inquired about how she was she would think, Just try and cross my moat. In a marriage you can close the doors and hide. It's usually not the vows we say at the start that solder us; it's what happens behind those closed doors over time.

· · ·

Noel had felt Anna's husband was a fine enough choice though he worried his daughter was marrying a boy more than a man. Girls will do that when their father is very strong, ironically, cede the central role to Daddy to protect his pride, or perhaps to protect his sense of place in his daughter's life. And they do it subconsciously. Human nature conditions us against understanding choices as we make them; emotion usually enters the equation long before intellect can have its say.

The morning after her wedding Anna woke up wondering if she'd made a mistake. She was standing by the stove in the chalet, boiling water for tea. A family friend came up and put his hand on her shoulder. He lived in Geneva and worked in finance. He'd driven up late the night before on hearing the news. He drove a blue Fiat Panda, a car Noel often teased him about, saying things like *Who do you think you are, Gianni Agnelli?* Though it was Noel who'd studied the Italian industrialist for style. Noel wore his Patek on the outside of his cuff.

"Would you like some help, dear?" the friend said.

"I can boil a pot of water, thank you." Though she wasn't even sure that was true, then. She knew only what was right in front of her, and as the peace that comes with close focus was the only peace at hand, she took it, who wouldn't. In those days, she could see a knife and know it was a knife. She could hold a knife in her hand. What action she might take if left alone with a knife was anyone's guess, though suddenly Anna wasn't sure she desired anything anymore.

"I meant this," the friend said, and held out his hand. "Help." There were two tiny blue pills on his palm. Anna took and swallowed them.

"Don't you want to know what it is?" he said, shocked.

"Not really." And then she said, "I can boil a pot of bloody water," and wiped her eyes.

The drawbridge was up. The moat was full.

148

Q.
A.

A colleague of mine had his offer of employment rescinded due to security concerns. It was rescinded two days after he received it. He tried to understand what had happened, what those concerns could possibly be. He considered appealing the ruling, challenging this sentence he felt had come down on him unfairly. When he inquired about avenues of appeal he was given a lecture that came down to *No más*. That same week a young woman was in my office, she had also received an offer followed immediately by a letter rescinding it. In both cases the rescind notes arrived before the polygraphs but after the test that asks things like, *Have you ever blacked out when you've been drinking?* As if I would remember. And things like, *Are you angry at dirt?*

Many people fail and go on to get jobs at other places, FBI, DIA. If you apply to those places, you of course admit you've had clearance denied by the Agency. And then those other places call CIA and say, *Hey, we're considering hiring this girl. Can you tell us about her?* And CIA says, *Um, no.*

It would be in the Agency's interest to start trusting its own.

Put me through bells and whistles. Throw me from a plane. Train me to lie and deceive. But then let me in the trust tree.

Trust inspires confidence. You want it if you're teaching tenth grade but you require it if you're placing your life on the line. Which might lead one to another question: What kind of temperament is drawn to the absence of trust in the presence of danger?

Beirut.

Her parents had ended their honeymoon in Lebanon, 1972. The trip came to symbolize some last happy thing between them. They'd first flown into Munich for a weekend with friends and then taken a flight to Hvar for a sail down the Dalmatian coast. From Dubrovnik they flew to Beirut. Those were the days of honeymoons like that, at once grand and bohemian, exotic. The absence of airport scanners. Her father knew how to sail though he didn't need to for this occasion; a friend had lent them the boat, a sixty-foot Swiss yawl, as a wedding gift.

After Beirut, they'd rented a car and driven to Tripoli. When Anna would say things like, "Tripoli sounds like an odd place to honeymoon," her father would tell her, "There's an absolutely spectacular beach," and Lulu would say, "It was work." The word "sailboat" didn't seem to match up with the word "work," though. What work could be done at sea, or on a beach? After her mother left, Noel would talk about that trip as a way of saying he didn't regret the marriage. How can you regret something that had once contained such joy. Anna wanted to understand if that trip was the end of something, or the beginning. She wanted to understand where the problems started. Children care about precision. Children care about the facts.

It was only later that Anna understood that facts are relative and subjective and that the order in which we receive facts matters. The order in which a story unfolds. Who is telling the story matters, too. If she'd asked Lulu about the honeymoon Lulu would have had a different view.

Munich, Beirut. Her parents were in these places only a year before the Israeli raid on Lebanon, when IDF forces landed missile-equipped Zodiacs on the beach. They were there only weeks before the Olympics and the Black September massacre of Israeli athletes. The raid was interpreted as retaliation for the massacre. If you look at the order of things, that interpretation makes sense.

Her father would often say that everything is coincidence and luck, that timing is incidental. Telling the story of the honeymoon was an opportunity for Noel to tell a story about history. Before she was ten Anna knew about the Mossad and the Baader-Meinhof gang, about Ehud Barak and Golda Meir and the iconic image of the black-masked kidnapper on the balcony inside the Olympic village, anonymity enhancing his menace. When Anna pointed to the picture once and said, "Daddy, does the man have a gun?" her father said, "He's not a man. He's a terrorist."

The trip was Anna's origin story, the days during which Noel and Lulu decided to have a baby, and the trip when they started talking about the lives they wanted to live, maybe the trip where Lulu told Noel she didn't want him traveling so much anymore, the trip where he realized that sooner or later cracks would appear in the glass. Anna always wanted to hear more about the yawl and the ports. She wanted to know about the crew and what they ate, and whether yawls have kitchens. She wanted to know what her mother wore at night and what one packs for a holiday that moves from the coast to the city. And why Beirut? "It's the most beautiful place in the world," her father told her. Though he would say that about many places over time.

Noel told her about the central square of Split and about the old stone walls of Dubrovnik. He told her about Lebanon and Israel and what had happened in the lead-up to that summer and why certain people wanted one thing and other people wanted another. He tried to help her understand that the reasons bad things happen aren't always evident, that diplomacy isn't algebra. He always encouraged his daughter toward empathy and away from judgment. He always tried to help her see a thing a different way. He wanted her to understand how everything in the world had changed that summer. The telling and retelling of the story became a thing between them and, like Heaven's rooms, it was a default for them in times of stress or times when they didn't want to talk about other things. Every family has these topics. Lovers have them, too. Your safe places.

"And why did you have the fight about when to leave?" Anna would ask her father.

"Your mother wanted to stay and see the Olympics."

"And you won the argument."

"She came around to seeing it my way."

Noel told her that the night of the massacre one of the Israeli athletes had sent his thirteen-year-old son to stay with his mother. In doing so, he had saved his life. The men who carried out the attack were refugees. "They came from camps in Lebanon, Syria, and Jordan," he told her. And then he would show her on a map where those places were. He would explain that fear, and a sense of injustice, often inspires bad actions. He would explain why the president of the United States had elected not to attend the athletes' funerals.

As she got older Anna would increasingly wonder about her mother's experience of that week. As those places took on new prominence in the world, she would think about the coincidence of her parents having been there when it all started.

"Who honeymoons in Tripoli," she asked Lulu when she was older.

"Your father."

"You liked different things," Anna said, delivering her conclusion.

"Well, if commitment counts as a thing, yes," Lulu said, delivering hers. After a certain age Anna didn't ask about Tripoli anymore. She didn't ask about the past.

Anna didn't know how often Noel and Lulu spoke after Lulu left but she had the sense they stayed in touch. Sometimes she wondered whether Noel begged her mother to come home. Maybe the separation worked for them though it had broken their little girl's heart. Until she was older, she couldn't understand. We don't think about our parents experiencing certain things until we experience them ourselves. Then we empathize, and forgive. Anna had developed a new interest in the details of her parents' marriage as the day of her own wedding approached. Had Noel gotten down on one knee? Had Lulu been afraid before she said yes.

Children care about precision. Children believe in facts.

Even when you're all grown up you're still someone's child.

What coincidence.

What luck.

Q.

A.

A polygraph is not a deposition. If you keep to yes and no on the poly, if you say only what's essential, you look like you are hiding something. Having something to hide makes people anxious, Anna, even a professional.

You have to remember that what happens before you're hooked up to the machine is also part of the performance. From the moment you enter the room, they are observing you, looking for slips. Once they turn on the machine it lasts only a few minutes. So you see everything leading up to turning on the machine is essential. What happens before you begin often sets the tone, even the outcome, of the thing.

The last poly I observed took place in a spectacular spot. I walked into a room in a hotel to realize it was the honeymoon suite, which amused me. There was Cristal, and a pound tin of caviar, on ice. There were flowers everywhere. The bed was on a raised platform.

And yet it was elegant, not tacky. It was breathtaking. It overlooked the ocean.

Through the window I could see people diving off yachts and racing on Jet Skis. In a honeymoon suite you tend to think about honeymoons, so I was thinking about how if I ever fell in love, this was exactly the place I'd like to come, though I could never afford it. I was thinking about the irony of how this would be my only time in a suite like this, and I was there not to love someone but rather to destroy someone, to question her allegiance to me, which would be to desecrate the trust. Once you question, things shift, and they did with us. But this was part of my preparation for letting her go and part of her preparation for leaving. It was understood.

I was there to oversee the polygraphing of my shiny thing, as some suspicion had arisen around her. I had been told not to tell her about the poly. I had been told to tell her only that we were coming to this place for a break, that she would be afforded complete cover to wander the beaches and read books, that no one would know where she was and that not even I would bother her, that this was a trip for her to have some peace away from what had become an increasingly stressful situation.

We had lunch. And then I told her I had to take her to a meeting, and when we arrived at the door to the suite I told her I was sorry but that we were going to have to polygraph her. She responded with absolute calm and professionalism. Though she likely had known the whole thing about rest and books and beaches wasn't real. She wasn't into rest anyway. A holiday for her was work and accomplishment. She was defined by her invisibility but also by her preternatural drive. That drive came from a rage she held against her family, against her father in particular, and I could guess at its origins though they were never disclosed.

Q. A.

The technician had flown in only an hour earlier. He shook her hand and then said, as he was organizing things, as if he were asking her the time of day or the temperature, as if it were beyond benign, he said, "I plan to ask you if you're committing espionage against the United States, if you are a double agent." He was drinking a freshly pressed orange juice from room service. It left a line of pulp on his lip.

"Understood," was all she said.

I wanted to make some gesture to comfort her then, but that wouldn't have looked right.

I wanted to tell the guys not to push too hard, that I believed in her, but that wasn't protocol, either. I wanted to rewind the tape of my life to that night at the Farm. I should have stood up and started running then and not turned back.

I was raging not only at the polygraph but also at being in that suite with no honeymoon and no girl and no prospect of either or even a way to think about how to get from where I was then to what acquiring those other things entailed. I was raging and the value of rage in those situations is equal to the value of anger at dirt.

"How much do you know about the polygraph process?" the technician asked.

"She's read the literature," I said.

"Yes," he said, "the literature," he got the joke, he understood. He placed the straps around her wrists. She was looking out the window, at the boats and the blue.

There is a new spectrum of discretion now, Anna, Instagram infamy on one end and solitary confinement on the other. You can't have it both ways. Our generation, we have to choose. And our generation can't choose solitary confinement. Your father could move through the world undetected, and it's possible he made allegiances that weren't always black and white. Gray doesn't sell well on a poly. Ironically, when spies discuss their personal lives they tend to be extremely candid. When discussing work, they will lie to your face. Or they will say something polite, which forces a pivot. On the poly, you find people speak at length about the most personal things, sex, religion, addictions. It's as if they want to spill the truth out in advance of what will inevitably be a necessary lie. Talking too much before the poly starts is a tell, in a way, the guys know to pick up on it.

"Have you ever committed espionage against the American government?" the technician asked her, and he was smiling as he asked it and she was smiling as she looked at me.

"No," she said. She asked for a glass of the orange juice. I could see that the lines on the poly were even, she had passed, it was over. We waited a full minute then I nodded to the technician and he flipped the switch, the machine was off.

"Nice work if you can get it," he said to no one in particular.

He was one of the good ones.

I gave him the caviar on his way out.

Playing Through.

In the last chapter of the video, "Christmas," there is a field covered in snow. There are two boys, brothers, wrestling in the snow, and the snow is still falling. The boys aren't dressed properly, either; one is in only a T-shirt, the other is wearing a bathrobe. And the snow is starting to fall harder, a blizzard in infancy. The boys look like they can't feel the cold, the threat of illness, the risk. They have no sense of danger yet. You don't have a sense of danger until you've experienced loss. Until you've experienced loss you have a sense of invincibility.

> *Yes there is a God. And in the room for joy there is a wide glass trellis that reaches all the way to Heaven, and woven on its levels are garlands of flowers, bougainvillea and wild rose and impatiens. Joy needs her space. Joy needs her space, darling.*

Anna played the snow scene over and over. It reminded her of her own childhood, of taking fiberglass gray sleighs and red plastic saucers to Central Park. She would pull the sleigh or saucer up the high main hill, the almost quarter-mile of open slope where everyone seemed to be. She was fearless. Other girls clung to their mothers while their mothers prayed their sons would return to them intact. Anna wanted to go faster than the boys. She wanted to be first to touch the rail of the fence on the far end of the field.

Only later, thinking back on those days while rain fell against the high windows of the loft where she lived with her husband, later, as the rain fell slant against the hotel room windows, only then did it occur to Anna that perhaps she hadn't been all that fierce. She simply hadn't experienced the loss that raises our tolerance for risk.

Do you love your daughter.
Of course I love my daughter.
Did you participate in the unauthorized exfiltration of an asset because she reminded you of your daughter?

Lulu's father had a diplomatic job at the American Embassy in Paris. Her mother ended up an editor at *Paris Match,* journalism once having been a more viable hedge against shaky financial foundations. The money was tied up then, in locked trusts for future generations and with cash-flow requirements for prior ones. Anna's great-grandparents had lived in a world defined by silver and staff and removal, by racing silks and Spanish trainers and summer trips to Saratoga, a world as foreign to Anna as Oz. And, in ways, as foreign to Lulu. Lulu's parents understood the imagery of it all but they'd left the horse farms and plantations and gone out into the world, refugees from the American aristocracy in its twilight. Lulu's parents wanted their children to speak languages. They wanted to take them to places where people didn't care where they were from. Lulu spent summers in Spain and Greece and Christmases in Istanbul and Cairo. At nineteen she was an American girl who never felt American, a Southerner who didn't understand the South, a girl who, when you asked her where home was, might have said, "I don't know," and meant it. And then one day she met a boy in a barn in Louisville and decided on the spot he was the one. He was a poet. He was a rider. His name came from his birthday, December 25. He didn't have a dime.

It took a long time to conceive, and when Lulu finally did, the pregnancy was not easy. "There will only be one, I think," she told Noel in her thirty-fourth week. A day later she was rushed to the hospital for an emergency caesarean. "He will be perfect," Noel told her, on the phone, with Anglican certainty. They started the IV, then the doctor hung the curtain up below her waist as the anesthesiologist placed a mask over her mouth and nose. Later, she told Noel the experience reminded her of a hunting trip they'd taken. They'd shot roe deer, and she'd watched while the men gutted them. "I think I know how the deer feel now," she told him.

Anna arrived weighing four pounds, ten ounces.
"Maybe she'll fight for justice," said Lulu, later, in the nursery.
"Maybe she'll just be happy," said Noel.
He was home from his trip. And he had changed.

The two boys in the video keep wrestling. The snow keeps falling. The scene runs almost three minutes. As Anna watched it, she suddenly could feel her husband come up behind her. She stopped the video. Whenever she heard the boy talking of the rooms, she heard Noel describing them.

And there is a room where you can find the people you have lost, it's a room for stories. In this room you can listen or you can tell a story of your own. Do you want to tell a story, Anna? Do you want to listen to a story of mine?

red, white, blue

. . .

"We're late, love," her husband said. He was wearing black tie. Sometimes Anna forgot how handsome he was, sometimes familiarity doesn't breed contempt it simply breeds blindness. He knelt down and put his head in her lap. He asked her to put her fingers through his hair. "I don't want to go out," he said, though he didn't really mean it.

"God, let's not."

"Duty calls."

"Can't we tell duty we're not available?"

He pulled her mouth down onto his. This was his way of saying, No, we can't. The kiss meant, One doesn't talk back to duty. Another fundraiser, another new set of views on tax brackets or the balance between security and civil liberties, civil liberties being what one of her husband's new friends called "terrorists' rights." There were a lot of new friends and they spoke a new language. Her husband now said things like, "A balance of civil liberty and security exists, but isn't weighted." He had taken on new habits, too, had cut his hair short. Anna understood from him that "everyone" was in a panic about November as there was no viable candidate for a critical Senate seat. She understood *viable* to mean someone the party was excited about. The old incumbent wasn't planning to run. The only challenger was riddled with flaws.

Who was everyone? Everyone included almost no one from his prior life. Everyone wasn't the artists. Everyone didn't live downtown in lofts or walk red carpets. Everyone was discreet and refined. Everyone watched the Sunday shows. Everyone, his new crew. And everyone would be there tonight.

"There is a room for stories," Noel would say. "And in this room you offer words to the angels and they tell stories using those words. What word would you like to offer tonight, Anna?" And if she couldn't think of one, he always had something ready.

Her husband looked at the open laptop, the frozen frame. "It won't bring him back," he said gently. He took her hand and ran it along his chin. His worry about her was spiking again. When his own father passed away he'd never read any of the condolence letters.

Anna hadn't told him she'd met the boy, the man, in the video. And she hadn't told him she knew the video was coming before it arrived. She never told him about Noel's vision of Heaven. When she was little, Noel told her stories about his childhood, her grandparents, his in-laws, history. Lulu's mother had a walled garden on Centre Island; Lulu and Noel were married there under a grape-laden pergola. He told Anna how her grandparents hid lollipops in that garden on holidays. They tasked the children with finding them so they could have time. "Alone," he told her. "They were always looking for how to be alone, they never tired of each other," he told her. Somehow that seemed an apt definition of love, one Noel never achieved.

Everyone is vulnerable.
I am not a spy. Because that is the question, isn't it?
Everyone is vulnerable.

And as she walked across the room to the closet, aware of her husband's eyes on her back, it occurred to Anna that her mother had likely played through scenes like this, too, scenes in a marriage where you don't say what you feel or reveal all the facts, where the withholding is a part of the love, a way to keep peace. Playing through, like in golf, which can be construed as an act of aggression on the part of one team or an act of grace on the part of the other.

"I love you," she said.

"What," he called out, still from the floor.

"I said 'garden,'" she said, and he laughed. And he looked at the laptop and told himself that whatever she was going through would pass.

Q.

A.

The intelligence community has been frustrated recently about all this media attention so they've performed hundreds of polygraphs trying to link employees to members of the media. This is a problem. You can learn a lot from journalists. And as the powers that be increasingly restrict who you can spend time with, the powers that be are harming the mission. China, Russia, the Islamic State—now we're going to add *The New York Times* to the enemies list? Yes, Anna, we are. Because the definition of an enemy is someone from whom we have something to fear. And they are afraid of the media. The new precautions, we all knew, were only going to trip up good, innocent people. One of the reasons things turned against your father was his relationship with the press. If you're skilled you can manipulate a journalist, and he did, both when he was in and after he got out. He could read an article and match its sources to its disclosures like a child matches an image of a cow to an image of a pitcher of milk. It was always completely clear to him who had talked, who had leaked, when and where and why. He was an aficionado of the art of betrayal. It was a gift. Until.

To define an enemy broadly, fine—but what about the definition of insanity? No one tells you in this business when you're at risk of going insane, so you keep doing the same thing over and over and expecting a different response. If that's not insanity, it's masochism.

Rain.

How had Anna met her husband. She'd asked her father to help her find a job. It seemed the best and worst option at the time. She'd missed the Princeton interviews for consulting and banking. She had no excuse for this aside from not having been interested in consulting and banking. Around April of her senior year she'd toyed with the idea of travel—an Asian grand tour followed by something ruthlessly serious and unassailable, like medical school. Only she hadn't done pre-med. She hadn't done pre-anything. Her mother said, "Just pick up and go, you'll find what you love," which sounded risky, so when her father said, "Let's have lunch at the Ford Foundation," she said yes. "You're perfect for us," said the chairman of the board, and hired her before the coffees came.

Anna would place all her Russian and Chinese to the side, for the time. She would wear something other than jeans. She would stay at her desk late most nights, considering water shortages in Mali or creative expression as a means to map and change poverty near Victoria Falls. She spent hours exchanging emails with a Zimbabwean woman who believed peanut-based energy shakes could help solve child starvation. Over time she would gravitate west and north, to

Niger, Nigeria, Senegal, and—in particular—Sierra Leone, work-ing with local activists to push political and cultural change. The men and women she met repeatedly astonished her, reframed her sense of her place in the world through the lens of their extraor-dinary experiences. "I don't think you do this because you want to end African suffering," Lulu said once, typically cynical, if not frank. "I think you do it to understand how people in situations of extreme pain process emotions, which is fair, which is perhaps an effective strategy." Anna's boss, Innocent, told Anna she had a rare talent. "You *listen*," he told her, "and listening is empathy and empathy is everything."

All this seemed vital and relevant. The work made her feel alive. She forgot about her love of literature and about the boy on the West Coast and the girl she'd wanted to be while lying in his bed. Once, she had missed him. Once, she'd regretted her choice not to follow him to LA. And more than once she'd conceded he'd probably been the love of her life. Then it all became too painful and indulgent. She would elect to focus on what was in front of her. Water shortages, corruption, drought, and famine, the kinds of things that tend to take the edge off a broken heart. The kinds of things that tend to open a heart over time.

The foundation's front doors opened onto its celebrated atrium, twelve stories of trees lined by glass, a jungle in the center of a skyscraper in the center of a city. Anna ate lunch alone most days looking up at all that green, considering grad school as a viable escape from bad dates and indecision. Alone, until the day he came and sat beside her.

"What do you do?" Jeans, cashmere blazer, hair like an angel. Anna thought about Lulu and Noel in the stable. *God, what is this,* she thought.

"I work upstairs," she said, suddenly embarrassed by her egg salad sandwich, her thick glasses.

"It's like eating in a rain forest," he said. "Only quieter. No wild beasts."

In all her years of working there, no one had once said anything about the atrium. No one had expressed joy or wonder. *People who work in the Vatican probably don't talk about the Sistine Chapel all day, either* had been her rationale. His knee knocked hers.

"Are there any beasts upstairs?" he asked, looking up.

"Lots. What do you do?"

"Oh, I'm just trying to change the world."

"Ambitious."

"I'm trying to get music to parts of the world that don't have it yet."

"Like rain forests?"

"Exactly. Though rain forests have their own music, don't they."

He held out his hand and said his name, "Jake."

"Anna."

"Anna in the rain forest, nice to meet you."

And he turned and took the stairs two at a time.

Game, set, match.

Anna had never felt anything like what she felt then. She tried to will it away, like a flu arriving at an inconvenient time. She didn't want to meet the love of her life yet. She wasn't ready. Even after all that rushing, she wasn't ready. It didn't matter. He would somehow find her number and he would call her that night and ask her out.

Q.

A.

The Agency was born just before the Cold War. Russia was our main enemy. Leaders at that time asked themselves questions like, *Will the Soviets exert their power over the world?* Or, *What does the Soviets' development of nuclear weapons mean for us?* Most sophisticated thinkers today, when asked what is our greatest threat or who is our greatest strategic adversary—say China. Only the thing is, Americans are very bad at long-term planning, and China is a long-term problem. Americans rarely plan past five years, this is politics but it is also human nature. Darwin might have called the American stance on security "survival," but I prefer the phrase "news cycle."

The Chinese don't have this problem. They plan ahead. It's absolutely obvious to them that they will be the next superpower. They don't believe Islamic terrorists will be around in fifty years, let alone a century. As Noel would say, Why stick around when all those virgins are waiting? As Noel would say, The phrase "secure the building" depends on your point of view.

Q. A.

In the army, "secure the building" means have your guys surround the building. In the navy it means lock the doors and keep the key. In the air force it means negotiate a long-term lease with low costs. And for marines it means make the building disappear. Everyone has his strategy. Everyone has her point of view. Ask me to secure a building, and the first thing I will do is ask you where the building is. My point of view is, location, location, location. Because if the building is in London or Beirut or Ankara, that's one thing. If it's in Beijing, that's another.

I was a loyal soldier, Anna. There were no wires strapped to my wrists when it was my turn to walk out. When my time came I simply disappeared. The last thing your father did before he died was not a crime it was an act of concision, and grace. Grace, the free favor of God, the salvation of sinners, the bestowal of His gifts. Grace. Anna.

Godfather.

"Your husband's going to run for the Senate seat, Anna." She was sitting in the dark little library of a townhouse on East Seventy-third Street, thinking back to that day in the atrium. Then, she'd thought *I'm just trying to change the world* was just a line.

She'd been summoned here by an old friend of Noel's, Edmund, a de facto if not de jure godfather, the one who had been at the White House for that state dinner. Edmund sat on the board of Noel's company, but the origin of their bond was the fact that they'd lived together at law school and then later lost wives the same year. They had helped each other heal, once.

Edmund found another wife, then divorced her, and then found a third, Edmund had survived and thrived; Edmund looked sixty at seventy-nine. And Edmund had been very focused on Anna since the avalanche. He would call and write and take her for long lunches or quiet dinners, where he would encourage her to work less and eat more. He'd send her tickets to basketball games, or the opera. He'd invite her out to the country for weekends. He was the kind of New Yorker who called Connecticut "the country." When she quit the Ford Foundation he sent flowers with a note, "Good choice."

Edmund's son, a neurosurgeon at Johns Hopkins, was exactly Anna's age but the dream of a match between them had never evolved past a high school kiss. When she heard the word "senator," it occurred to her she would have really loved a neurosurgeon. So serious, saving lives. Though neurosurgeons are as prone to narcissism as any music producer or politician, aren't they.

Edmund's library walls were lined in dark green fabric. Hunting prints hung in rows suspended from silk ribbons, additions of the new wife, to Anna's amusement. Her godfather didn't hunt and probably hated those prints but rules loosen in later marriages, or perhaps simply later on down the line. The second wife had liked new things and the third liked old ones, and eventually Edmund didn't care. His defining trait was his evenness. He was happy as long as he knew what was happening in the world and as long as his Rolodex afforded a role in it. He loved jokes, and Anna had heard him tell his favorite one a hundred times. It was about marriage.

"I have these friends," he would say. "They have the perfect marriage. They signed a contract early on indicating that the wife would make all the little decisions and the husband would make all the big ones." Whoever was listening would then ask what defined a little decision. "A little decision is something like, Where do we live or how many children do we have, how do we manage the money and where do we spend holidays?" And whoever was listening would ask, now sensing the joke, what then defined a big decision. "What to do about the Middle East, of course. What to do about China." The joke always got a laugh, though Anna's response to it was visceral, as she saw some truth in it. She guessed this had likely been the story of her parents, in the beginning. Somewhere along the line maybe Lulu had wanted in on the larger decisions. Or maybe it was Noel who changed. One of them had altered the contract.

As a teenager Anna had smoked cigarettes out the windows of the townhouse with the future neurosurgeon. There was a fireplace with a Rubens above it, surrounded by gold and crystal bowls of candied ginger on glass nesting tables. Edmund was always occupied, it was rare that he summoned her. "Even Warren Beatty will one day be eighty," he told people when they remarked on his stamina. In the last year alone he'd flown to Africa with Interpol to track elephant poachers before ending up in Dallas to mediate a dispute between an NFL owner and his offensive-line coach. Apparently a lull in the action now afforded him time to get her husband into office.

Anna listened to everything he had to say before giving her view.

"It's just preposterous."

"It's absolutely not, given current conditions."

"Is current conditions a euphemism for his money?"

Anna guessed that the reason she was being told the news in this way was to take the edge off her reaction, to prepare her to believe and to behave. She wished her husband had told her while his head was in her lap. The fact that he hadn't indicated he was afraid of her.

"Is he afraid to tell me himself?"

"I asked him to let me talk to you first."

"Am I that unruly?"

"Simply softening the blow. This is not quite what you signed on for."

Anna thought about the decisions, and the contracts.

"He's not a politician."

Edmund took some ginger from the bowl. He knew the challenge at hand was not an argument he had to win but rather a set of emotions he had to navigate, and order.

"He's not a politician. What would you say are his gifts, Anna?"

"He's very good at parties, with people. He is very good at spotting talent."

"Yes."

"He has an endless appetite for new sources of affirmation. He's a workaholic. He's an idealist."

Edmund said nothing.

"But he can't win," Anna said.

"With my help I think he can," Edmund said. "It's a game of branding, really. And this cycle is a fluke, there is really no competition."

"Branding?"

"Branding and money, fair enough."

"When is the election?"

"November." It was June. "Anna, he has it all."

Noel had loved politics. He would have loved the idea of his daughter in this role. He often told people his one regret was never running for office. He always said the only thing you regret is the thing you do not do.

The Rubens was an ink drawing of a child looking down.

"Why am I here?" Anna asked.

"I need to know you're not going to leave," Edmund said.

And while Anna thought about that and about the viability of becoming pregnant if their lives took this turn, he added, "He only has it all if he has you."

Q.

A.

You never have consecutive tours in the same place. They don't want you losing perspective. They don't want you falling in love with that country. In the old days, and I mean the really old, golden days of diplomacy, an envoy would be dispatched to a city. And it might quite likely be in a region for which that envoy had a pre-existing passion. A country or continent the envoy had knowledge of, perhaps even had family or emotional connections to, perhaps he had studied its history in school or spent a university term there. It's possible the envoy had spent his entire life hoping to live there one day. In those days, when an envoy was dispatched, he would learn the local language. He would often marry a local girl and become deeply tied to the town. A dream come true, what's better than that. Though at some point in these cases there often came a time when the envoy began viewing his true country as the place he was stationed. Imagine visiting China in the 1800s and your ambassador arrives to welcome you wearing a Ching dynasty robe. Suddenly, he might not be the finest representative for the United

States anymore. People said your father fell too hard for Asia, that his love affair with Asia was the death of his love affair with your mother, the bending of his moral compass. I say people are jealous. I say Noel's love for Asia taught him who he was. That's true love.

Senator.

She'd selected a dress for the press. It wasn't a color she otherwise would have worn but seemed suitable considering the occasion. Her husband was announcing his intention to run for senator of New York. And though on that morning he had two formidable opponents for the primary, one would be indicted after sexual assault allegations then the other would drop out for reasons that were never quite clear. Politics was always a game that seemed at once rigged and unpredictable; a new era defined by rage, and Twitter, made it all the more so.

At thirty-six, with no prior political experience, the election only months away, he was tagged by the media as arrogant and absurd on the one hand, audacious and impressive on the other. Jake didn't have a chance, the papers said. He didn't understand the party machine, he hadn't kissed the rings. Though the outcome of the race didn't really matter to the candidate; winning was never his goal. The choice to run wasn't about Senate reform or a love of his adopted home state. The choice was a play to change. Once the race was over, Anna's husband would no longer be what he had been before; he would be a viable member of the political elite, someone engaged in serious things. Once the race was over, he could play on an entirely new field.

And this was how the donors and the party had pitched it to him. The party operatives saw a chance to make their careers with this charismatic long shot, an untested candidate, a true nonpolitician, a creative founder of a music company fresh from sale. He was young and he was bright. In ways he was the perfect candidate for an era where charisma lapped experience.

The night of the announcement Anna sat quietly in a corner, considering the hem of her dress. It was lined with tiny suede embroidered daisies. When one of the young handlers offered her Perrier, she asked for a Heineken. She looked at the man she had married and considered the fact that he didn't have a chance. And yet there he was. Risk never bothered him. Anna thought about her childhood, the eggshells, about being in a place that felt safe. She fingered the daisies and told herself it was time to focus on the present. Her husband was having a tiny microphone clipped to his lapel. Tonight was the end of the era of eggshells.

"What are your *interests*?" asked the campaign manager, who sat beside her, who looked all of twelve.

"Interests?" Anna said.

"You know, hobbies, skills, likes and dislikes, do you cook or whatever? Chess?" He had a sense of humor. "We can't assign profiles until we know who you are. People will want to know you," he said. He liked the Zimbabwean story. He liked the Phi Beta Kappa.

Anna felt an arm slip around her waist. The candidate was wearing a suit, which he had about twice a year until now, now it would become the uniform. Anna had always envied how easy everything was for him, how he could move an idea from inception to launch with the bat of an eye, placing the right rolled calls. How he could throw on a shirt and look like a god. How he could say he would sell his company and pivot and in six months they were walking out into a blitzkrieg of cameras. She experienced life as a climb. He experienced it as a fast skate across fresh ice. In either case, of course, one can fall.

The Ford Foundation phoned. They wanted her back. Princeton called. Would she sit on the board? Old friends emailed, Let's have lunch, come be partner, what's it feel like, are you free for opening night of *Bohème*? "A surfeit of honey," Noel would have called all this, by which he meant lots of sweet stuff, options, deal flow. The phrase also meant decadence—excess. It wasn't quite a compliment.

Lulu called to ask if it was true and whether Anna wanted her there for the announcement.

"That's kind of you, but no," she told her mother.

"Do we think he knows whether he's really a Democrat or a Republican," Lulu asked, drily.

One of the aides opened the doors to the hotel suite that had become their temporary home and motioned to the candidate that it was time.

"I love you," he said, and lifted her hand to his mouth. He looked right at her. "Can you hear me?"

"Yes," she said. She closed her fingers around his wrist and held tightly. Then someone clapped and suddenly everyone started moving. He slipped his wrist free. He moved ahead of her and staffers closed the space between them. "Here we go," she could hear him shout out, to everyone and to no one in particular.

Q.

A.

You don't have many hobbies as a case officer. You acquire the hobbies of the source you're developing. Your versatility in acquiring new interests is critical to your success. You have a source who loves soccer, you watch the World Cup and maybe even learn to play. You have a source who loves beer, you become an expert in European microbrew technologies, perhaps it turns out you're related to the Anheuser-Busch family, maybe your roommate in prep school was a Stroh. And you are developing these new skill sets and passions while under the cover of your day job, so your days become busy. You build the architecture of the larger lie of who you are through the architecture of the little lies, your likes and dislikes, your desire to become the person your source needs you to be. This illusory architecture is in service of the mission. This architecture is the mission. You're constantly learning new cover details, Social Security number, grad school girlfriend, favorite French film or modern novel or sculpture in the Louvre. This is increasingly how you spend your downtime, memorizing who you are about to become, forgetting who you once were. Memorize, forget, memorize, forget. Repeat. At any one time you will have five to ten different mobile phones for five to ten different yous. At night, you will lay those phones out in a line on the desk or the coffee table or even the bed. You remove the batteries. One of those phones is the one that may ring if there's a bomb threat. One is the one that rings if an asset is in trouble. The phones are nannies for children in your care. That was tradecraft, Anna, a table full of phones.

A table full of phones is not a life.

If you have only one asset and one phone, then that's one you can never turn off, the one from which you can never remove the battery, never not acknowledge when it rings. It becomes the source of everything. A device. Or, more precisely, a voice on the other end of a line you can neither predict nor control.

Fish.

"Marines are skilled at suffering," said a man in uniform seated at the head of the table.

"So are debutantes," said the hostess, seated to his right.

It was a fundraiser for Jake's campaign, hosted by people she didn't know but who had arrived at the inner sanctum of their lives recently by virtue of a check they'd written, and then by further virtue of subsequent checks they'd inspired others to write. They were "bundlers," people who took pleasure in matching political candidates with sources of funds, like casting directors matching actors to parts. There was an art to it. It wasn't just who had cash, not at the highest levels, and especially not in this case, with an unorthodox candidate and urgent time frame. It was the quality as well as the quantity of the money that mattered, and bundlers speak of funds as being deployed, like soldiers in a time of war. This particular couple was known for opening their opulent home as a kind of deployment, and it didn't disappoint. They'd purchased two double-wide brick townhouses on either side of a city block, with a garden running in between them lined with wild roses and a slim, sunken lap pool. They believed in God and country. They believed Jake's opponent was a criminal. They believed the outcome of this election was critical.

"America is at a tipping point," the hostess said in her opening toast. "We needed a deus ex machina and here he is." She made a motion with her tumbler to the candidate. Anna's husband rose to speak. They had stayed up late the night before, going over what he would talk about.

"Don't forget humility," she'd told him.

"What's that again," he'd teased. The last weeks had been a lesson in how quickly things can shift, how suddenly someone who has been unknown in one context can become central, how there are second acts in American lives and here they were, having theirs.

It was only a dinner "for ten," which meant ten thousand dollars per person, not ten in attendance. Anna still believed her husband would lose and that then they'd be back to their old lives, easy anonymity, the absence of "seasoned" advisers minding each choice.

The decadence of never caring what anyone else thinks.

There was no more decadence now.

Once upon a time the candidate had admired his bride's irreverence, it came in such contrast to what he called "the rest of the package." Those who knew her well accepted irreverence as an essential part of Anna, what separated her out in a sea of other girls who had gone to certain schools and been trained for a certain kind of life. Those circles of early privilege interlocked to form an impenetrable fortress, well armed against entrance of the new, though occasionally exceptions were made. It was a club, and clubs were one thing Anna had always rejected. It was genetic.

It would have been far less stressful to belong and oblige but Anna had never belonged. And then she had married someone who always belonged because of his confidence, his ease—then, a bunk bed at Brown; now, this palatial city home. Circles didn't apply to him, he moved straight through them. Perhaps he didn't even see they were there, and in rendering them invisible, denied them the power they held over others.

Fish.

. . .

Anna lifted her eyes and saw her husband was looking right at her. He had finished his speech and was mouthing the words "How did I do." This was rhetorical, he knew how he did, and his nod at needing affirmation was for her, not for him. And as a way to indicate she understood, Anna excused herself from the table and stopped by his place to give him a kiss behind the ear, then to pull his face toward hers with one hand to say, "You got the A."

The powder room was wallpapered in gold leaf. White linen hand towels hung from a low glass bar by the green marbled sink. By the toilet was a little bamboo table with old *Vogue*s and miniature black basalt sculptures. They were like the sculptures in the hotel bar in France. Here, they were leopards. There, they had been Roman gods.

Her mind went back to the restaurant that night.

"Do you fish?" he'd asked her, just before the cigarette flick.

"No."

"That's a shame. Do you know how to catch a fish?"

"A rod?"

"A rod, that's very funny."

"Is this the part where I am meant to ask how one catches a fish?" Anna said.

"Well, this is the part where I tell you."

"The right rod?"

"The right bait."

He made a motion with his hands, casting an imaginary line.

"Oh, *fishing*," she'd then said loudly, acknowledging the imaginary line. She was also acknowledging that something was being said and something else was being left unsaid. And that was when he said her name, Anna.

"Wait, what," she said. How did he know her name.

"Anna. Not for the literary echoes."

She returned to the table and the topic was a rumor of the opposing candidate's failing health.

"It's a blood disorder," someone said.

"A crack in the stained-glass window," the hostess said.

Anna had a desire to question the debate at hand, to say what worried her about the campaign or its potential effects on her husband and her marriage. But she behaved through the last course, through espressos and freshly baked brownies, through the tour of the art in the apartment and last lectures on her husband's infinite potential. She behaved all the way into the town car that was now always waiting for them, even on nights like this, when they were only blocks from their hotel, even as she'd protested and asked if they could walk. She behaved into bed and was about to open a book.

"Let's talk," her husband said. He pulled a chair up to her side of the bed.

"What about?"

A second rumor had arrived that night alongside the checks and the foie gras.

"A political campaign is a hothouse for rumor," the hostess told Anna as they walked around the house after dessert.

"Why is that?"

"Rumors metastasize in the presence of power. A rumor sends a stone through the stained-glass window."

She was placing Anna on notice.

A rumor was headed toward her window.

Q.

A.

You're constantly collecting information about terrorist attacks, about how they're trying to kill you. Obviously falling in love in that context, there's a little carpe diem that sweetens things. But love cannot thrive in the presence of constant, clear danger. Over those years in Asia I wasn't in any condition to marry anyone. And yet you long for connection. And so the desire to couple up and share a life can be replaced by a will to couple up and save one. It happens every day. And seeing someone as like your own daughter might be an even harder emotional matrix to break free from than seeing someone like a lover. A man will always see his daughter as a little girl, even once she's all grown up. A man will always defend and protect her, even when she makes poor choices. And even when she places a system at risk. Lovers come and go. Daughters are forever.

Rumor.

"Please," Anna said, sitting up in bed. She looked at the blue curtains. She didn't want to look at him. "Please tell me." She pulled the shirt up over her knees and pulled her knees to her chest, like a child. "You're scaring me. And that woman scared me. Did I do something?"

He was staring at the ceiling, twirling ice in his gin with a straw.

"I love you," was what he said, and looked at her.

"I love you, too, you idiot."

"What did Noel do for a living?"

"He worked at a bank."

"At a bank."

"He moved money around, whatever, maybe he owned the bank."

"There's a rumor he was a spy for the Chinese."

"That's preposterous," Anna said, and as she said the word out loud she remembered the last thing she'd called preposterous, the idea of his running for office.

Her husband slipped the straw in his mouth and waited, giving her time and space to process what he'd said.

"That video."

"It was nothing. Some case officer cleaning out his desk."

"Well, you might want to clean out your desk now, darling."

And he gave her a long and loving but firm look.

"Let's clean out the desk."

"Of course," she said.

And in that moment Anna didn't see Noel in the high-backed chair she saw the boy chasing the falcon over dunes and she heard the man's voice by her side on the rocks saying, "Rome is provincial, Paris is provincial," and she saw the two Asian women in their blue silk dresses with the flowers. Those white buoys.

Her husband put his glass on the bedside table. He turned to face her. He traced the lines of her face with his fingers. He never tired of her. He trusted her completely. He knew she would not place them at risk.

"My better than wow," he said.

Q.

A.

In all your interactions with the Chinese, they arrive to meet you in pairs. If the Agency tells any overseas intelligence partner with the exception of China that we want to talk to its chief terrorism analyst, the other agency will say, Sure, of course, what time. Not China. The Chinese have what are called barbarian handlers, a select set of intelligence officers accredited to deal with CIA. The barbarian handlers are the gatekeepers, Anna. And so when CIA tells Chinese intelligence we want to talk to their chief terrorism analyst, China tells us we can speak to the handlers and they will decide. They call them barbarian handlers because we are the barbarians in their eyes.

I served ten years in Asia and it took me ten years to understand this. After a decade I could look in the mirror and see what they saw, the barbarian. Once you truly begin to see things from their point of view you can begin to question your own. You have to move radically outside of what you know to have this experience. Noel did that. He saw the barbarian, too.

The God Thing.

There exists, however, a God. And the long hallway that leads to the room where you will see that God exists is lined with the people you once knew.

What would it be like to have such certainty. Most adults Anna knew were unsure about God. Her own upbringing had been classic lapsed WASP, which is to say more eggnog and egg hunts, less birth and death of Christ. God rarely came up at Princeton or at industry parties or at the Ford Foundation. Anna had lived most of her life entirely insulated from any ideas of faith that were not abstract or ceremonial. Her friends were more interested in what happened last night than in the possibility of an afterlife.

She and her husband rarely talked about belief though they'd exchanged traditional vows in front of that fireplace, as if reciting words from a book neither of them understood or had read would solder the thing, make the marriage real. Elevate. "You are now spiritually responsible to each other," the minister told them. "He's exceedingly spiritually responsible," is what the campaign manager would say later in response to being asked about the candidate's faith. When asked if the candidate and his wife prayed together, he said, "Personal prayers are private."

After the rumor came a threat on the candidate's life, speaking of elevation. It arrived in the form of a letter and it accused the candidate of being a shill for the Chinese. The letter listed his Asian business interests and detailed his late father-in-law's extensive work in Asia as evidence of un-American leanings. Circumstances required them to take it seriously.

"Some people want to come and ask some simple questions," said the campaign manager, closing the door to the three Bureau agents waiting in the foyer. He said it as if he were talking about nursery school teachers, as if the questions they were going to ask her would be along the lines of favorite color or toy.

"Some 'people' meaning some federal agents?" said Anna.

"They're just here to talk," the campaign manager said. "We're just crossing *T*s."

A security detail had been hired and stood in the hall.

"Dotting *I*s?" Anna said.

"Right, yes." He was nervous.

Anna increasingly had the sense she was only an actor in a film now, one in which she was given the script one page at a time. She could feel the control she'd once maintained over her life slipping away. Her husband saw it differently. He felt he was placing himself in the hands of experts as a means to an end. Strategists, researchers, details. A chief of staff, federal agents, a chef. In his view, everyone around him now was there to assist in his rise, close the polls in his favor. He believed the letter threat was a distraction and told his wife not to worry. "Every politician gets one of these," he told her, eyes wide. He always saw the bright side. The first round of interrogations was benign; the threat was assessed as low. Still, the detail was kept at the door.

The God Thing.

As fall arrived, the candidate tailored his tastes, Budweiser replaced bespoke bourbon and gin, out went the Porsche. He disclosed his net worth. He listened to junior staffers' complaints and memorized the names of high-level donors' grandchildren. He got fierce on issues where he had once been lax or agnostic, like education reform and the minimum wage. He went to bed early and woke up before dawn to run the reservoir with policy scholars and City Council members. And he almost always handled little errors, except for one time, in the Bronx.

"Do you believe in God?" a reporter had shouted from the back.

"I'm not averse to Him," said the candidate, smiling, on the assumption his charm could eclipse the emotions of others. Not this time.

After, in the car, when Anna tried to explain why you don't say you're "not averse" to God, he didn't listen. He turned away. She had the sense she was chiding not the man in front of her but rather a former self of his, one no longer available to her. That former self had left the room of their relationship. It wasn't a lapse in their love but rather a shift in the chain of command, in the structure of the thing that had been intimate once, the thing that had included only the two of them. Now there were handlers. Now there were rules. Now, protocol. Anna could still see and feel his former self, bounding up those atrium stairs, the boy who wanted to change the world. She could still see him staring up at stars by the Statue of Liberty, feel him pulling her back into bed on hundreds of mornings, asking shyly for more, helping her to be happy. Could she catch that former self before he slipped away entirely, could she place him in her pocket until this race was over, then pull him out intact?

That night, he went to her and pushed her hair behind her ear.

"It's getting so long," he said. And then, "You're right about the God thing." He told her Edmund had called and said it was reckless not to have a view, said what kind of adult operates without clarity on faith. Not one who wants to serve in the United States Senate. "You were right, baby," he said. "Why don't I always listen to you?"

He was back, for a moment. It was enough.

He had engaged in more introspection in those months of campaigning than in the entire rest of his life, and it was changing him. And the nature of the change was unexpected. Anna was seeing the man she loved and once believed she knew do something truly radical: grow up. He was questioning his choices as deeply as she had once questioned hers. At the start of their marriage she'd wondered whether he had what it would take to grow with her. She worried now he was asking himself the same thing.

Q.

A.

He didn't care about money, Anna. You know this. Money was never his metric. He would fly first-class to Doha, but that's not a crime. Once, when his hotel upgraded him to a suite, he went ballistic. He cared about perception, about optics and rule. He would tell me things I initially found superficial. What jacket to wear on a certain occasion. Where to get my hair cut. But he also taught me that these things link into a larger set of expectations and strategies, the fastest way to inspire trust, how to break down a difficult decision into a series of manageable choices. He believed the most important choice we make is the people we choose to love and trust. He chose me. He chose her. We were delivering intelligence but we may also have been serving a second role, protecting his legacy. Maybe we were insurance that what started in that Chinese jail would be completed. There is no real end to the life of an asset. At the end of a career like that, where do you go? There is no home. She was facing a life of nowhere to go, and he understood. He helped me break down a difficult decision into a series of manageable choices.

Interrogation.

When the men from the Bureau returned, they had a new line of questions. The candidate and his wife were happy to oblige, a time was set, food was ordered for the room. There were three men, and they started by asking the candidate about his childhood, about his parents and his school and the choice to leave Brown, and about the early backers of the company. They asked about the rock stars he knew and certain parties he'd attended, about the more serious drugs he assured them he had never touched. They asked about affairs, only to learn that there had been no affairs, and about social-media slips, of which there had been one or two. *Have you ever stolen something?* was one of the questions, to which his response was, *Only Anna's heart.* He was whistle-clean. It surprised the agents, as it might have anyone, to learn that this candidate, who seemed to live fast, was actually slow, and thoughtful. He was a businessman who had done well and wanted to give back.

"There are so many different ways to serve your country," the candidate would say, as the party-appointed advisers had trained him to say, when people asked why he was doing this. His narrative was one of redemption. He was a man who had seen there was more to life and wanted a change.

Change is admirable.

Change inspires.

And then they asked about his father-in law, about the Swiss funeral and who was there, and they asked if Anna had opened all of her condolence letters. And that was when she elected not to tell them about the video.

When Anna sat in the same chair in the same hotel room a day later, everyone knew what the skeleton was or might be. It was weeks after the dinner where the marine had discussed suffering, almost a month after the night when her husband had made and remade love to her after acknowledging the rumor, refusing to leave their one safe space exposed to its flicked lit match. He had held her so tightly that night.

There exists, however, a God.

Whatever came after, the man she'd met had once been the little boy in those dunes, in that snow. He had once been someone's son. He had provided Noel with his vision of Heaven.

"Did you meet with anyone identifying themselves as an employee of the Central Intelligence Agency?"

Anna said nothing. He had never mentioned the word "CIA." He had never mentioned the phrase "case officer." The word "CIA" did not appear anywhere in the video.

"When did you meet with him?"

They placed a photograph on the table and asked her if she recognized the man in it.

Anna looked at her husband and he nodded, giving permission to go ahead and tell them everything. Anna knew the nod was also acknowledgment that whatever she chose to say or not say, he loved her.

Q.

A.

The "it" factor in this world is so simple. It's likability. It's charm. It's empathy and the ability to connect, to see another person clearly and have her truly see you. This connection creates confidence. Only the problem is that you can't teach these things. You can't teach a person how to convey confidence. It's usually genetic, and by the time you're memorizing Virginia maps, you either have it or you don't. You can teach someone Arabic, you can teach him how to fish. At the end of the day what differentiates you in this line of work isn't teachable. Teachables are icing, Anna. In some cases, if you're beautiful, you get chosen. Sometimes it's just a beauty contest.

Wonderland.

"We believe he assisted in the exfiltration of a Chinese double agent."

The news had come hard to Anna but harder to her husband, his waxing self-absorption channeling everything now through the filter of the polls. What effect would this have on the election, if it was true? What effect would this have on the baby now keeping them up nights, the new baby, which is to say, the campaign?

"We believe he assisted in the exfiltration of a Chinese double agent and we'd like to understand why, and who helped him, and who stood to profit from his choice."

"Profit?" her husband didn't understand the use of this word in this context.

The men who came after the Bureau agents came from the Counterespionage Group at CIA. They explained to Anna that her father had worked for CIA in various capacities for almost three decades, operating under nonofficial cover. They told her how Noel had mentored a young American case officer stationed at the U.S. Embassy in Beijing. This had all come before, and then alongside, the glass office, those deal toys, the "placements" and the structured products, the end of the marriage and the cycles of new girls.

"We have reason to believe he may have worked in the service of a foreign government."

Anna had seen the screens charting the status of stocks on Noel's desk. She couldn't recall anything about China in their lives, aside from that one state dinner. She was so little, though, it never occurred to her to ask. It rarely occurs to children to consider their parents as people, too. Anna had absolute faith in who she believed her father was. If ever a man told you who he was when you met him, it was Noel.

"He recruited a Chinese asset and she has gone missing," they said.

Does she remind you of your daughter?

"My father is dead," Anna said.

What is your daughter's name?

"He mentored a young case officer and he has also gone missing."

Asking him about Anna was a trick, a way to elevate his heart rate, a way to open him to saying more, to slipping up. Even an expert can trigger an avalanche.

"Noel is dead," she repeated.

Would you like for me to repeat the question?

"Has she contacted you? Has he contacted you? We believe you would be an obvious choice for—"

They were trying to trip her up.

"My father is dead."

Angels. Angels are off-limits.

Anna asked the men to leave her alone with her husband.

"Do you love me," she asked; it was rhetorical but it was safe.

"With my whole stupid heart."

"What should I tell them?"

. . .

Later, one of the men placed a photograph on the table.

"I only met him once," Anna said. Which was not true.

"When was that?"

"Almost a year ago."

"Can you be more specific."

"He told me he thinks Paris is provincial."

In the photograph the case officer wasn't poised to dive off rocks or looking up at stars or rolling through dunes with a little brother. He was lying on a bed in a hospital room. He looked different, though she couldn't tell if the photo was taken yesterday or a year ago. The man tapped a finger on the photograph.

"Don't you want to know about him and what he did, Anna? Don't you want to learn more about the plans your father set in motion, the man your father was?"

And so she went, Alice down the rabbit hole.

Q.

A.

Goddesses can come in many forms. Noel always told me things rarely look like what they are. He told me, "You won't see her at first." The image she projected was of someone who would evaporate into ether if left unprotected, someone with no impact on the world around her. And, *voilà*, she turned out to be sui generis. She turned out to be our Einstein, our Galileo, take your pick, the one whose intellectual gifts equaled her appetite for risk. Or for revolution. The one who comes along once in a generation and changes everything. She was our most critical source in the most critical part of the world at that time.

The heart demands attention at the least convenient time. When we tell our heart to shut up and wait, the heart says, *Saving the free world, motherfucker.* And then we don't have a chance. We will feel a thing up against all instincts not to. In these cases there is nothing intellectual. There is only emotion.

Shiny Things.

Maybe it began with that first visit from the Counterespionage Group, or maybe before, with the murder board brought in to assess the extent of the damage. Maybe it began with her husband's decision to run for office, maybe when she opened the video and fell in love with the little boy and his rooms, with the idea that there is always an innocent beginning, whatever the end. Or was the start of this story when Anna fell in love in the atrium, buried her father, lost a baby. Is there ever a clear start to a story?

There were soon other visits from other people in what everyone in DC called the IC, the intelligence community. This obsession with codes and acronyms struck Anna as not only silly but inefficient, everyone always having to explain what they were talking about and who they were "with" all the time. Everyone who came claimed to have a stake in her "story," as they called it, though she might have preferred the word "trial." In the absence of evidence to the contrary, a theory had emerged around Anna. The theory was that she had been the last person to see the missing case officer and that she must know where he is, that he must have told her something at that meeting, that he must have arranged to see her again and that

she would be willing to believe in him because her father believed
in him, too. What crimes had he committed? What promises had
he made?

Anna didn't want to interfere with her husband's dreams. They
were her dreams, too.

"I don't know him," she told one after another of her
interrogators.

"You did meet with him, though."

"Yes. Once. As I said."

"And what did he say?"

"I don't remember."

"Did he make a plan to meet again?"

"I don't remember."

"What was he wearing?"

And Anna saw the swimsuit and the outstretched arms. She
saw the cigarette flicked across the dark sky.

"I don't remember."

"Did he mention China?"

There was the woman from the Senate Select Committee on Intelligence, who seemed keener on Anna's view of the election than
on any missing case officer. There was the former deputy director
of operations, who opened the minibar as they talked and proceeded to empty it over the course of their conversation, M&M's
to IPA. And then finally there was the former director of Central
Intelligence. That meeting didn't take place in a hotel room or an
office. It took place at Edmund's townhouse. They were less than
two months out from the election, and the dials of discretion were
rotating right. Dials of discretion or of panic, depending on your
point of view.

The former CIA director immediately put her at ease. He told her, "You're on my watch, Anna. No one is going to hurt you. We only want to know what you know."

"I don't know anything," she said.

"I only want to help you make the right choices."

He promised the current levels of intrusion into her private life would end soon. He was calm and precise and presented himself as her advocate.

"People in my world are always chasing shiny things," he told her. He was standing at the window. She could see the park beyond him. "Is that a Rubens?" He walked close to the mantel and admired the drawing. "Do you like art, Anna?" He wasn't looking at her. "Your father always said the art world was just another drug war with better-looking dealers."

"Will I need an attorney," she said.

He turned around.

"Nah," he said. "Let me tell you a story instead."

Q.

A.

So much of what is done is classified, accessible only on a need-to-know basis. Most of the time you don't even see what happened in cases where you were involved. Information is quarantined, and silo-ed. Eventually, the silos become impenetrable. When you're in, you hear a lot about this or that senior guy, what he's done. Over time you learn that so much is timing. As opposed to, say, expertise. In many cases someone was simply in the right place at the right time. Noel once met a North Korean nuclear physicist, the ultimate shiny thing, *by chance*. The physicist walked into a bar and Noel was there talking to a beautiful girl. The Korean wanted the girl. That's not art; that's accident. Noel's opening the line to the girl evolved into recruitment. Once a Russian rang the Bern station to talk to Allen Dulles when he was a spy stationed there. Dulles had a tennis game with a pair of gorgeous Swiss sisters, and he wasn't going to miss that, so he didn't take the call. And so the Russian took a train to St. Petersburg to start a revolution. Espionage is the art of wise choices. You choose to talk to a girl at a bar, or not. You choose to meet that Russian, or hit balls with those Swiss sisters. Bond gets Swiss sisters *and* a revolutionary. But Bond is a myth.

Metaphors.

The story the former director told Anna was about a little boy who was stuck in one place.

"*Stuck* is a metaphor," he said. He had moved from the Rubens to the couch. He had crossed one leg over the other and was swinging a suede loafer off his foot. He wore red socks, like the pope. The story was about how an old woman sees the boy and offers him rice and a map, then leads him to a door. The little boy goes through the door to a new life and becomes a kind of king.

"Is *king* a metaphor, too?" Anna asked, thinking of kings and golf, of Roosevelt and silencers.

"The thing about being king, it kind of kills your ambition," the director said.

"Yes."

"All the boy wanted was to see the old woman and thank her."

"So she comes to the palace."

"She comes to the palace and he offers her everything and she says she alr—"

"She already has everything she needs."

"Exactly. Did he tell you this story?"

Anna thought next he would tell her the story was about her, her husband, the campaign. She was wrong.

"The story is the story of your father, Anna."

"What?"

"He was once given a bowl of rice."

"I don't understand."

"We only want to talk to the man you met in France."

"I think 'met' is ambitious," Anna said.

"He went to France to find you."

He told her about the arc of his own career, how he had started out in Saigon as a journalist. He told her about Tony Poe, a marine who trained Laotian tribesmen during the Vietnam War. Poe operated in Bangkok and Burma, training Tibetan Khambas and Hui Muslims for operations inside China. "He claimed he was the one who led the Dalai Lama out of Tibet."

"Why are you telling me this?" Anna said.

"You should assume anything you were told in France was a lie."

The silencers, the kings. *Practice.* Is it possible to trust someone you've met only once?

"What's an exfiltration?" Anna asked, without looking up. She was taking his play and running it, testing the waters of his trust. She could talk like these people. She could speak in code and riddle, too. And she had cleaned out her desk. She had nothing to hide. She had only questions, not answers, and felt entirely entitled to raise them.

Q.

A.

I knew the guy who planned the exfiltration of the Dalai Lama from Tibet. He was famous for never taking notes. "That's what memory's for," he would say. I asked him once if he had total recall and that was when he told me the story. I remember asking your father about it. "Paper is primarily for historians," he said. This view was of course counter to the culture of the place, the pathological reporting, over-briefing, of review, review, review. Or was it. Perhaps there were two cultures, and only one that was codifed, only one that was paper, lists, history, mineable for romantic reporters. The idea that you could plan a sophisticated op absent paper was a revelation. And a template.

Occasionally a case becomes so sensitive that a cable goes out that says something like, *We're actually not meeting this asset anymore.* It will say, in black and white, and likely right under the word "classified," *This asset has been terminated.* Only this is not true at all.

What is true is that the asset has become more essential than ever. The cable claiming she was terminated is called "eyewash." Eyewash smokes out the fear and risk that renders an asset vulnerable by claiming they no longer exist. And from the time that eyewash is distributed, the case has become restricted handling.

Money.

A thing can be kept quiet if managed properly.

The campaign carried on. Nothing was said about what was happening in their personal lives. Nothing was said about the fact that an investigation had been launched, that it was related to the Central Intelligence Agency, that it was related to the father of the candidate's wife. Once, Noel had been the model citizen and a kind of happy ghost hovering over the politics. Now he was being accused of espionage. Everyone was closing ranks.

The campaign was going well. The major papers had endorsed him, and so had two ex-governors. The mayor appeared with him in public in Queens, Brooklyn, the Bronx. And money brought more money. "Fundraising is a self-licking ice cream cone," one of the high-level donors said. The candidate's gifts bloomed in the shade of acclaim. On camera, he was incandescent.

At the hotel, the interrogations continued. Endless rounds of questions punctuated only by breaks for coffee and air. Had she known her father had worked in China on behalf of the U.S. government? Had she known her mother knew the man she had met in France, had in fact fed him meals in her home many times? Did she recall ever meeting him as a child? Had he been in touch last month, last week, this morning? Does she have an email address or a phone number? Did he carry a phone? Did he carry two? Did he give her anything?

Saying, "I don't know" a hundred times is tiring.

Saying it two hundred times, you forget what it means.

Q.

A.

I once had an asset who was very greedy. He flew from our meeting, in Munich, directly to dinner with the Mossad in Paris. He wanted to work for them, too. And he told me that. It's a little like introducing the idea of polygamy into a marriage, a blow to your confidence if you're the first wife. I had discovered him and in his way he was very valuable. I had assessed him as someone we could trust. That's the gold standard of being a case officer, Anna, your ability to assess others. Though CIA can assess you, they can't assess your ability to assess others. There is a leap of faith there. In other professions the central skill set is rigorously tested—consider the banker, the sniper. CIA trains you and then sets you loose. Sometimes a very good person provides very bad intelligence. And sometimes a monster gives you exactly what you need. Noel was never afraid of the monsters. He'd take Iago over Hamlet any day.

Joni Mitchell.

They call them problems. The German Problem. The Russia Problem. The Islamic State Problem. And now, if there was a counterespionage problem, Anna stood at its center, increasingly spending her days in hotel suites answering questions about things she knew very little about. Her honeymoon, apparently, had been the scene of a crime. Technically, she was there of her own volition. "You're free to go," one of them always would say. This was said for the record as everything was recorded now, formalized; nothing was casual. Casual was from another era. "BC," her husband called it. "Before the campaign." As in, *That was six months BC.* Before campaign. Before crisis.

The candidate was having his hair cut in their suite's galley kitchen. Someone sent a barber from a shop on Lexington, as everything now was about saving time. "Baby," he said, joyful, nodding at the barber-to-go. "You're just performing your civic duty. This will all be over soon."

She sat on his lap and laid her head on his shoulder.

"I'm sorry," she said.

"You are only trying to keep him close, that's what you're

doing," he said, and she welcomed that view, whether it was for-giveness for her choice to lie, or something larger. Ambiguity and elision didn't scare him, another trait she might have listed when considering his future as a politician.

What is civic duty, anyway, and what are its limits? Is it a crime to keep a thing private? A life isn't a law class, open for enroll-ment, structured to educate and illumine. A life is emotions, rela-tive bases for comparison, instincts, survival, chaos. In her final round of interviews Anna told two guys from the Bureau that, yes, she had met the man in the photograph at Cap d'Antibes, and not only that, she had met him not once, but twice. She told them she'd met him first in the bar at the hotel and then, later, outside the restaurant by the water. She told them about the weather and the lobsters, about the menus printed in French and Russian, the latter for the oligarchs, and about the dress she had worn, which was new. In a state of exhaustion, near despair, Anna finally elected to tell them everything—almost.

There are some things that can never be said.

The interrogation was coming to an end.

"Did he ever mention a location, a meeting point?"

Anna thought about the silvery fish her husband caught on August trips to Alaska. Don't the salmon ever learn?

"Is there anything else."

And Anna looked over them and out the window. She saw nothing but clouds.

"No, there is nothing else."

Q.

A.

What's the definition of a crisis?

In the old days, everything was cables. Cables require work—encryption, printers, *decryption*. And so they inspired concision. Fewer words meant less work. Old cables on even the most critical and complex subjects read like tone poems, as in TIMBER SYCAMORE, UPDATE. As in PLAYA GIRON, MAYDAY. Or PLEASE REPORT FOR POLYGRAPH. Today you have texting. Today you get an instant message telling you it's time for a poly.

It's easy to slip up in an instant message.

Maybe in the poly they ask if you've ever leaked sensitive information via text message. And, as you believe you have not, you deny it. So they ask again. You deny it. They keep asking and you keep saying no until you begin to question your own interpretation of events, or your sanity, you begin to doubt your own recollection of the content of that text. You start to wonder if this will all end if you simply say, "Yes."

Yes is a mirage in the desert, Anna.

Q. A.

If you're indefinitely suspended as the result of a poly, you can't travel or work. You're told nothing about your case. Indefinite suspension is like a bomb threat. Faced with the threat of a bomb, people act irrationally. Faced with the threat of a bomb, you crawl to the mirage.

Grenade.

It had to do with interrogation techniques. That was what cracked her, exploded the grace. That was what elevated everything. They knew exactly what they were doing. They always do.

The counterespionage team had returned. They had declared in advance that this would be their last visit, the last interrogation. And then there was no interrogation at all. They had arrived only to tell her it was over. Jake was in the room, and she heard him catch his breath.

"You're done," they said, and Anna's husband put his hands over his eyes.

Then, while one of the men started in about national security and the "origins of single-scope polygraphs," about Noel's brilliance as a businessman and the candidate's chance at a win, Anna looked up at the ceiling. She wondered if the recessed lights obscured bugs for sound. She looked at the mirror over the mantel, and wondered if it held a camera. What would it take to design a room so that everything within it was recorded? What would it take to make a place safe and clean?

One of the men said something about sheets with high thread counts and Bonne Maman jams in silver cups, about the Château Lafite in the minibar. "No enhanced interrogations took place in rooms like this," he said.

Her husband sort of half rose up, a gesture that would have been chivalric if he'd carried it to conclusion, but he didn't. He was now living in that place of willed ambivalence posing as stances taken, a place absent emotional resolve—politics.

And for a moment the clean, safe room was silent, as if a grenade had been rolled across the floor. A joke coupling French jams and enhanced interrogation was a kind of grenade, still pinned, still palmed in the hand of the assassin. A threat. It meant, We are more dangerous than you are. It meant, You're in over your head. It tapped Anna's central fear, of being seen as something she'd spent her entire life trying to escape.

What do you do with all your rage. You embrace it.

What comes after BC?

Later, when they were alone, Jake told Anna he was going to win. His opponent was dropping out, apparently there was a family issue.

"Also, they love our story."

And part of Anna wanted to ask, Which story is that. The story of their marriage. The story of his spectacular conversion, Saint Paul of Brown, and the Boom Boom Room. Was it her silent, graceful demeanor, her privileged impenetrability, the sex appeal of scandal. Or was it simply that they were new.

And she closed her eyes to try to see what was coming next, but all she could see was black.

And then she remembered what comes after BC. Of course. AD.

Q.

A.

Paranoia is a common theme in the literature of espionage. What inspires acute paranoia is the thing you don't know. Something at close range you nonetheless cannot define. Something you're experiencing but cannot source. Why am I under investigation, for example. Visitations from a witch, for another. Hunger in the absence of food. Paranoia is purely protocol in spook life.

I had to accompany a diplomatic pouch once, an acute exercise in paranoia. The pouch can hold a diamond or a diplomat. It's the principle of immunity in transit. The pouches are not subject to investigation, or search. Governments use them to send things back and forth through their embassies. I wasn't cleared to know what was inside it that day. I wore it strapped to my wrist. I flew Jakarta to Singapore to Tokyo to San Francisco to DC. It could have contained weapons. It could have contained a shiny thing.

The poly technician sometimes travels with the machine inside a dip pouch. When technicians travel, they cede home-court advantage, they tend to get paranoid, this shifts the dynamic. One might wonder if it skews the results.

Toys.

"He caught the bus," Edmund said. "The dog caught the bus."

He was talking about the candidate, this now all-but-certain, impending victory. He was looking around the suite, someone had sent in a rack of dresses for Anna to choose from. A television ran news on mute in the background. Everything was the election, everything was the ramifications for the state, the rise of a candidate willfully exploding party expectations and poised to color outside the lines, a candidate not opposed to God, a candidate who loved his wife and who built and sold a business and came from nothing and seemed to have it all. Edmund looked at the television. The crawl mapped weather, and exit polls.

"It's really a philosophical question, isn't it, what happens when the dog catches the bus. What does the dog actually want?"

Anna felt like telling Edmund that if her husband was the dog, then he had been the one driving the bus, but she didn't, and Edmund went on. "Is the dog catching the bus a fairy-tale outcome or a nightmare?" It amused her to see him in a state of mild shock, and joy. The toymaker when his toy soldier starts to walk.

Anna had invited Edmund to the hotel. She wanted to understand the things she didn't know. She thought Edmund could explain to her what was happening. And also, Edmund must know the history. "Your father always wanted to go to China, Anna. In school he wrote an essay about Asia, how he hoped to learn from it by traveling there." Anna remembered Noel's advice on entering Princeton, what he'd said about how understanding China was essential to understanding the world. "Travel to China wasn't easy in the old days, especially in his line of work. When he heard some of his colleagues were heading out to Beijing, he asked permission to join their trip."

In his line of work. Some of his colleagues.

Anna was picturing the rows of Lucite deal toys. At lunch at her father's office there was a lady who came around and ordered takeout, whatever you wanted. Anna once asked for fries from one deli and a shake from another, testing limits, as little girls do.

"And what else," Anna said.

"He was told that the answer to his request was neither yes nor no."

"Well, he never took no for an answer."

"Never. So he took the request to someone more senior."

"And."

"And he was told that the answer was neither yes nor no. Which is sort of how they talk there, or did at that time. It wasn't such a big deal, it wasn't like he was doing some high-level national security work, Anna, he was having fun, it was meant to be a short post-Virginia thing, serve the country and all that, he knew he would have to leave and go out and make money, that was always the goal."

red, white, blue

.   .   .

Money is not the metric.

He wanted freedom, is what he really wanted.

She was nine that day at her father's office when she'd gotten her shake and her fries, and when Noel found out, he was horrified. *You are the last person here who can act like a princess,* he had said. The next time she visited, a shake and fries from those two different delis were waiting for her. Noel's carrots always lapped his sticks.

"He was finally told that if he wanted an answer he would have to have it directly from the director. The day before your father walked into Stans Turner's office, Turner had fired eight hundred employees."

"That sounds like a lot."

"Your father was fearless. He walked right in and asked to go to China. Later, an aide told him he went to China because Turner thought he had guts."

Edmund walked over to the dresses. "These look expensive," he said. "Maybe too expensive."

"He was fearless," Anna said.

"He spent more than a week in prison," Edmund said, turning around to look at her. "And, as you now know, he got to know another prisoner. Who happened to be one of the wealthiest men in China. Later, that other prisoner introduced Noel to his family, to his children, and to his granddaughter."

He pulled one of the dresses from the rack. It was white.

"This one, I think," he said. "What do you think?"

"And then what?"

"And then what depends on your point of view. Only no one really knows how Noel ended up in that prison. Did the Chinese government set it all up? Did we? Who really gave him that bottle of alcohol? Who sent him into that square? There are no accidents, Anna."

"I don't understand."

"I believe your father thought he was doing a good thing. I believe he followed orders. And I believe everything that came after was real. He built the business. Maybe he had help. Everyone gets help somewhere." He put the dress back on the rack and looked at Anna. "God, he loved you. That was true."

Anna stood up and walked to a wooden chest of drawers on the other side of the room. They would be moving that night to a larger suite for the final lead-up to the election. A silk robe was folded on top of the chest. She thought about a bath.

"Maybe he helped the girl because he thought she was in danger."

"I don't care," Anna said.

"Maybe he helped her because she reminded him of you."

"I am going to take a bath."

"She hated her family and she wanted out of China. She spied for us, and then she made a deal. Noel was the one who brokered the deal."

Anna could see the silver cup, her gift engraved with POET. Perhaps it wasn't his favorite deal toy after all.

"They have theories, but no facts, now. They have optimal outcomes, confirmation biases."

"Was the avalanche an optimal outcome?"

"The avalanche was weather."

On the TV screen, riots in Denver, Dallas, Philadelphia.

"You're about to become very visible," Edmund told her.

"Yes. I'm trying to decide if that's a fairy tale or a nightmare."

"I loved him, too, you know."

Anna walked over to him and kissed him on the cheek. "I know you did." And then she said, "Don't worry, I'll behave."

Q.

A.

.

Have you ever received conflicting weather reports and as a result found yourself unable to make a decision? It happens all the time. One says, *Clear, highs of seventy.* And the other says, *Ice storms.* One says, *The actions you're about to take have been vetted and authorized by legal counsel.* One says, *Use your judgment and don't fuck this up.* Conflicting expert opinions can be disorienting. Perhaps at times that's exactly the point of having experts.

You don't want to end up in a Chinese jail, Anna.

It turns out both men were being watched. The officers who arrested them did a strange thing, placing the American and the Chinese in adjacent cells. Or not strange at all, there are no accidents in China, perhaps there are no accidents anywhere in our world. It's possible the Chinese government sent that man to find Noel. That Chinese man gave your father extraordinary information in that jail, information that expedited Noel's rise through the ranks, which afforded him the option to carve out the role he served.

Some say information that afforded his fortune.

It's possible that during those days in that prison the Chinese offered Noel introductions to several powerful Chinese families, ones that still seed the highest diplomatic ranks and who send their sons and daughters abroad to Harvard or Princeton or Yale under pseudonyms. Perhaps Noel promised to help with the Harvard kids. A kind of godfather—de jure, if not de facto.

The question they asked your father the day of the avalanche was not whether I was a spy, Anna. The question they asked was whether he was one.

You will receive conflicting reports.

It's only weather.

You receive them, you make choices, you let go.

Lock.

"Let's," he said. The candidate, high on joy, was running his hand over Anna's belly. The polls were in, things looked increasingly like a lock. "I want," he said.

Q.

A.

Espionage is lonely. In most cases you're the only one who has ever met your asset. How she is portrayed, impressions others have of her, it's all up to you. It's up to you to portray her how you see her, up to you to prepare the reports of what she's said. Once you invite another officer into the equation, you're giving up control in exchange for a kind of confirmation of your work. This loss of control is brilliantly built into the system but it comes at a price. At a certain point in the lifespan of every asset someone else will meet her, take her over, run her. This "turnover" is a kind of tragedy and an affirmation. The failure or success of a turnover is a critical metric by which you are judged.

Blood.

Five, four, three—and then the cameraman held up two fingers, then one, and then Anna was live on the local news discussing the election. She was wearing her uniform, a slate-gray pantsuit, a light pink blouse, choices that had been vetted and voted appropriately feminine, unintimidating. And apparently also "true to who *you* are." That's what the campaign manager had said when Anna walked into the studio, his PDAs buzzing in their holsters.

There were three correspondents seated around an oblong glass table, two men, one woman. Anna barely had her earpiece in when they started asking questions.

What's it like to be married to someone so dynamic?

It's never boring.

Is your husband a revolutionary?

I prefer the word "rebel."

What does he do to relax?

He plays the piano.

What do you do to relax?

I listen.

Are you surprised at his success after such a brief time in this field?

Not really, no, he tends to come and conquer.

.   .   .

Though even as she tried to be calm and maybe even on the margin amusing, Anna was thinking about the day her father died, perhaps as a hedge against anxiety or more frightening thoughts, the way you think about rainbows while being rolled into Anesthesia.

Conditions were spectacular then, and she'd gone backcountry skiing with a guide all morning while Noel drove to the airport to collect his guests. He had told her some business associates were coming for lunch to discuss his commitment to a cause. Her guide had said how proud he was of her recent improvements, and when they'd reached the peak and the sky started darkening, he'd dared her to race him down one last time. She was winning until, on the final hill, she hit a slick of ice and fell, nicking her chin.

She arrived at the house as three men were leaving.

They walked past her without introducing themselves, then one of them turned and, utterly affectless, said, "You have blood on your face."

Q.

A.

If things go wrong, wherever you are in the world, cash is the sine qua non of contingency. If things go wrong it will always cost you, Anna, and so you will want access to cash. At the start of running new assets you set up what's called a pledge account for them, the parachute they use in case of—

You arrange these accounts often enough for assets that eventually it occurs to you, Why not set one up for myself? You're only human. Your asset needs a parachute in case the plane's engines explode; don't you deserve one, too?

You will hear your father created a sophisticated pledge account for her, which was fine. And you will hear he created one for himself, too. You will hear his entire business was a kind of vast pledge account, built on the backs of trades he made through his Asian relationships, all spokes leading to the center, which was Veritas. When you hear all this, Anna, what will you believe? Does it even matter what you believe if you loved him?

Mylar.

She'd approved the purchase of two thousand Mylar balloons—red, white, blue. Mylar is kind of frightening, she thought, observing all the young aides entering Astor Hall. One was so thin and holding so many balloons Anna thought he might float away. So much shine. There was something about it that seemed ostentatious, "too expensive," as Edmund had said, about the dresses. Couldn't they have simple old-school balloons? The campaign manager ran them all on short leashes now and had made most of the choices about this morning. He had instincts, and had become someone on whom even Anna relied. Edmund had started calling him Ice, short for "Ice to Eskimos," also short for "In Case of Emergency." In case, he could clean up a mess. He had navigated the presence of government interrogators in his candidate's suite and later he had navigated their removal. He handled death threats as if he were ordering takeout, never getting emotional, never irrational, always clear. "End zone, end zone, end zone," was his mantra. He was about getting everyone down the field. That day, when she arrived wearing the dress he had chosen for her, he took one look and issued his assessment: "Touchdown."

Everything was football, everything was winning, everything was forward momentum. His aides feared him, and though Anna had feared him once, too, he had grown on her and she had learned from him. "Red for you," she said. "For America!" he replied, though he was being ironic, he wasn't an idiot. He had his own cynicisms about this process and this country. When the candidate arrived, they gave each other high fives, like schoolboys. But the campaign manager was no boy, he was Machiavelli, as capable of philosophical quip as he was of casual slaughter. He was the one who had pulled Jake aside after an appearance on MSNBC where the candidate referred to F. Scott Fitzgerald's line about second acts in American lives. "Fitzgerald didn't mean it like that," he scolded. And he explained that the novelist was referring to the classical theater's three-act structure, where the first act established the players and the second act developed the ideas and the third and final act brought the crisis and resolution. "Americans *skip* the second act, Americans have lost the value of ideas." He let that sink in before adding, "Which is why you have entered this race, and why you will win." And the candidate thought that was brilliant. Anna found it equally seductive and alarming.

It was her husband's choice to deliver the acceptance speech at the New York Public Library. He felt the choice communicated an air of elegance but also of democracy—"elit*ish,* not elit*ist,*" as he put it. He had asked Anna to consider speaking, too, but she'd declined. He'd enlisted the help of friends; there would be a pop star singing, a Harlem children's choir backed up by the artists he'd signed for the label he'd sold to finance this campaign. And in his speech he would talk about the power of music. He would quote Dylan and end with the Billie Holiday line *people don't understand the kind of fight it takes to record what you want to record the way you want to record it* and the people would love that, immediately understanding he was describing himself. They would love everything about him, this man who had committed sins but was now devout—not about God but about them, about committing to their needs, about bringing back some dignity to politics. They would love his wife, love the glamour of her money, which was old, and the equal and opposing glamour of his, which was new, and love the note of intrigue, as it had leaked to the papers just that morning that Anna had been interrogated by members of the intelligence community. Scandal lent her new complexity and, given the current environment, any infiltration of government into personal life elicited sympathy. One headline was SHE'S NOT THAT BORING AFTER ALL.

In his speech her husband would talk about his love of America and his love of his wife and his ambition to change the world. The absence of children onstage would be an elephant in the room. And when Mylar rained down on them, he would whisper in Anna's ear, "You're free to go now." It would occur to her that that was exactly what you're told once you know you can never leave.

Q.

A.

They say the true mark of a fine case officer is an asset who continues to provide excellent intelligence after that case officer is gone. This is why we raise up our baby assets into fully formed adults, ideally no longer dependent on us. Assets are needy, though. Assets are only human. They trust not only you but also the idea that you will place them in the hands of someone after you who will take care of them. When your father gave her to me he gave me very clear instructions, too, Anna. And so, even as it was against the rules, whatever that means, I never made noise when he would want to be in touch with her. Everyone colors outside the lines at some point. And for years I didn't lose sleep over any moral ambiguity involved in it all. For years, I didn't feel. When you feel, it's all over. When you feel, you don't line up phones on the table; you smash them into the wall.

Celebration.

Back at the hotel it was close to three a.m.

"Like old times," her husband said, winking at his watch, which he held up for her to see. Though old times didn't include the security detail stationed outside their suite. Old times didn't include suites.

He hadn't touched her in weeks. *There hadn't been time* is how he would have put it, and meant it. He believed there had not been time. *There hadn't been desire* is how she would have. As they entered their rooms, they were not yet alone. The campaign manager embraced her awkwardly. He started saying something about statistics. "Fuck luck" was his philosophy, a way to counter the prevailing view, which was that in addition to skill there had been a holy load of luck and chance. The donors who'd given that early dinner, the one where she'd hidden in the powder room, arrived. They brought magnums of Dom Perignon wrapped in fitted glass-bead-covers. Waiters placed them on ice alongside Frisbee-size tins of caviar. *My man of the people,* she thought.

Her husband was trying to make it clear that the night was over, that he wanted privacy. He was trying to be firm but the others weren't having it. No one wanted to exit his orbit. He had become one of his artists. His art was ideas.

Anna retreated to the bedroom. She thought about her father, her mother, lollipops in the children's garden, and lobsters at the Cap, about other nights in her life that had qualified as celebratory. She thought about the former Agency director and the story he'd told her. She thought about her husband's view of God and Noel's view of Heaven and its rooms. What would he say of the room she stood in now? Was this the room for mercy? *This is the room for victory and ambition,* she thought to herself, and she wondered if those things were meaningful to Noel; he had never seemed to care, but now she was seeing him differently.

As she washed her face she could hear doors close, the others exiting. She could hear her husband moving to the bedroom. She was needy now. Intimacy would be a relief. Only when she walked back into the bedroom, she found him lying on his back, eyes closed, two tumblers of Champagne untouched on the table. CNN was on and they were talking about him, a phenomenon she'd ceased experiencing as surreal. The speed with which the press had accepted him amused her. They didn't know about yachts in New York Harbor or maybe the yachts didn't matter anymore. His team had successfully walled off his valorous qualities from all the excess. And she knew him so well and she was, and was not, surprised to be in this place. She was, and was not, surprised to hear him touted as a "future president of the United States." The future president was exhausted.

She turned off the television. She drank down one of the glasses. She sat next to him, eating ice cubes from the ice tray and watching him as he slept. She removed his tie and unbuttoned his collar. She placed her hand on his chest. She could feel his heartbeat. She knew now he was playing with her, and she knew her role. She leaned over and gently pressed a slice of ice into his mouth with her tongue. He opened his eyes. And they celebrated.

Q.
A.

The finest assets are not actually the vulnerable ones, the ideologues, the ones who believe they are working in the service of their nation against corruption. The finest assets are the ones who say, *Wire my bank.* They're businesspeople. Noel understood this. He was a businessman, too. And when he introduced me to her, the first thing he told me was that she was a businessperson. She looked the part. She wore the suits and had the degrees, she spoke seven languages. She was centrally set up in the most elite Asian social and political circles, easily Google-able via her institutional affiliations, all the right clubs, touch points. She was a covert weapon hiding in plain sight.

Noel had met her when she was only a girl, earnest, intellectual, unsophisticated. By the time we met in a bar in Beijing, a decade later, she'd grown up. She'd seen some very dark things.

In China Ops, it's forbidden to ask after assets once you turn them over. Noel knew a part of her was attracted to the powerful, narcissistic men she spent time with—for us. The men who told her things. The men who would eat her alive and leave her bones on the plate, if they knew. He was right to worry about the choice to recruit her; if it went wrong, it would go very wrong. And so when the time came he was right to help.

Mac Bundy.

It's hard to name a thing. Sometimes we don't call a thing what it is in order to protect it. An emotion. Or an idea.

"Oh, it was just *Mac Bundy*," Lulu would say. She would say this whenever something came up that was cryptic, something that people didn't want to discuss or name, like an illicit affair or yet another Wall Street scandal. "It was just Mac Bundy" meant "That conversation is closed" or "We don't have to talk about it anymore." It meant "The answers to these questions are above our pay grades and a matter of national security."

It was also an inside joke, as Lulu knew Mac Bundy and Noel had worked for him. It was Bundy who Noel looked up to, wanted to be like. Noel's own father was never remarkable in Noel's eyes, though he had been a kind man and had worked his entire adult life in the same small local library. Noel had developed his love of literature from his father. His father was the opposite of being out in the world, but he knew the world well from what he'd read. Noel never wanted to work at the local library, though. Noel wanted to be a Wise Man. He wanted to focus on the big decisions. Noel envied Bundy's place whispering into the ears of presidents, his role in rooms where questions of national security were determined. Mac Bundy had once run the Ford Foundation.

Lulu would tease men she met in government or national security about how they were always finding new names for what they did. When asked what her husband did for a living during those years, Lulu would say, "Oh, I can never keep track." Or she would say, "Oh, something to do with Mac Bundy." She would point out that one of the places Noel worked was simply called the Group, then later called the 303 Committee before being reanointed the Special Group and then evolving into the 40 Committee, the Operations Advisory Group, then the NSC Special Coordination Committee. Reagan replaced that with "National Security Planning Group," which stuck.

" 'National Security Planning Group' actually sounds like what it is," Lulu would say. "Can you imagine taking over thirty years to sound like what you actually are?" All Lulu ever wanted was clarity.

It's hard to name a thing.

The person she wanted clarity from the most was Noel. And he never gave it to her. Not long after Anna was born, Noel shut down to his wife. Without explanation, he let his heart simply close up to her. And in the process of trying to find an opening, Lulu bored holes.

By the time Anna was born, the language surrounding intelligence operations had become positively Soviet in its structure and sound, and that wasn't an acceptable irony anymore. You could imagine a historical moment when it became clear, a moment where everyone knew what was going on, knew that their government had evolved a sophisticated apparatus for covert action and that we, the American people, needed to accept that there were things we would know and things we wouldn't. We would also need to accept a third category of things: things we didn't want to know.

"Oh, bless and release," Lulu would say, when questions arose about where Noel was and what he was up to. "Mac Bundy," she would say.

Anna never experienced her mother's increasing sadness. Little girls track the grander themes—Mommy and Daddy are together, or they aren't; we live in a house, or on a farm; I have a dog, or a pony. Anna never internalized the tensions between her parents. She only experienced her mother as being there one day, then not there the next. Her mother had left her, but she would be all right, she would be loved, she still had those cracked eggs, those rolled-up sleeves, those visits to the Met and the White House, Toblerones and teddy bears. She had a father who was present and adoring. She was blessed. Anna's gratitude eclipsed her fear, which was that one day she might lose something else.

Anna hadn't thought about Mac Bundy in a long time when she received an email the morning after the election. They hadn't slept much, and her husband's head was resting on her chest. "Play with my hair," he asked, and she did with one hand while scrolling emails with the other. He often slept like that, curled in a ball and leaning on her. And there it was, between at least a dozen other subject lines that read "Congratulations," one that read, "It's Your Mother." It was an announcement of arrival, and it was all in caps, like she was shouting. I AM SO HAPPY FOR YOU. HOW ABOUT I COME FOR CHRISTMAS.

Anna had to laugh.

She put down the phone. She ran her hands over his face, tracing the lines of his nose and mouth. "He's my Achilles' heel," she'd told *The Wall Street Journal* in a joint interview they'd done for its *Magazine*. The journalist asked Anna why she'd been willing to accept the campaign, a public life. "Because he's my Achilles' heel." And her husband had leaned over and said, "How about just Achilles." In that moment, he could have asked her anything and she would have given it. She sometimes wondered if he felt the same way, if the power of that fit took two.

"Question," he said, and raised his hand. He was awake.

"What's that, *Senator?*"

"Was it all a dream?"

"Yes," she said. "And now my mother is coming for Christmas."

"Is she bringing Mac Bundy?"

He always knew just what to say.

Q.

A.

An *exfiltration* is when you covertly sneak someone out of a country, Anna. An exfiltration is a last resort. It's when your chief of station says, Situation Normal, All Fucked Up.

Every station has what's called an "exfil referent," the point person on those operations. The job of the exfil referent is to prepare the plan, the If Things Go to Hell, Then What to Do list. This person analyzes how we will get an asset out of a place, and you can imagine that pending the complexity of the place, the political environment, pending any travel or weather restrictions—it's a complex task. It's a little like those men who imagine life in the wake of a nuclear bomb. Their data shows the likelihood of a nuclear attack is low, but you still need a plan.

What's it like to be the point person on disaster? It's lonely. If the rest of the station had to spend time considering what-ifs with any seriousness, they would go mad. Who wants to think about worst-case scenarios all day long? You have enough going on. You're saving the world from global jihad, tracking assets, trying to recall your last bar tab.

A failed exfiltration is a stain on the station. Remember what John Kerry said, how no one wants to be the last man to die for a mistake. A failed exfiltration is considered a serious mistake.

Orchids.

Back at the loft, there were flowers everywhere. Black lacquered pots sat on her pine floors in long, neat lines, a nod at new order. The loft was the place Anna always would call home. It was the place they had fallen in love, after all. What better definition is there for home? She begged him not to sell it and, for a while, he complied. It was understood and accepted among the press that this was her place and that this was where she liked to spend her days as the evolution of their lives sped up. Someone had said something to the paper about her love for orchids, and suddenly they were living under a prolonged tsunami of cymbidiums, dendrobiums, phalaenopsis. Her husband teased her about having a verbal Midas touch. "Can you tell the *Times* we like French wines?" he said. Or, "Please let the *Post* know I need a new longboard." She felt the pots looked funereal. The black struck her as severe, but lacquer was the rage. All those orchids needed water, so much water.

His political risk statisticians had been wrong, as had the early liberal pundits. It turned out Anna was his finest asset; the voters loved her. Their love increased in elegant, precise proportion to her retreat from them, or was it her retreat from him, a willingness to give her man up to them and to their demands, a willingness not to want. No one knew what she wanted though they all asked. *Will you be taking a formal role in your husband's office? No. Will you be announcing a cause you intend to pursue? No. Will you be going back to the Ford Foundation? No. No. No.*

December was descending and soon Lulu would be, too. While Anna remained icy, her mother was treating the whole reappearance as a religious experience, one in which she herself was the prophet. "You need me now, darling." That kind of thing. And, "Thank God I can help," apropos of a new home in the city and another down in Washington. Only Anna wasn't a little girl anymore. Lulu's choices had freed her daughter. Her choices made it all right for Anna to take what she needed from her mother and discard the rest. There is power in discarding the rest.

On the very day Lulu was set to arrive, an unusual subject line appeared in Anna's inbox:

PAINT A STARRY NIGHT AGAIN, MAN

All those men had told her if he was ever in contact, to call them immediately.

They had told her she should have nothing to do with him.

They had told her he posed a threat.

You can never really clean out a desk, can you.

The marriage was intact. The baby question finally had been put to rest. Emotions were aligned and she even had started to think about working again.

It was a time for quiet and order. This email was chaos.

And all those cymbidiums, dendrobiums, and phalaenopsis in their black lacquered pots. They needed water. This email was water for her.

She knew she would open it, and what it would say. She knew what her response would be.

Q.

A.

Six weeks before her exfiltration I was alone, it was Christmas Eve. I had a little tree with white lights. I remember wondering what the hell I was doing, if I had the appetite for risk this thing would require. I was thinking about my childhood, how on Christmas Eve we would exchange wishes for the coming year. My wish that night was easy. I wanted her out, safe. Christmas morning Noel phoned. He asked if I knew what *deus ex machina* meant. And then he said, "Because I think we're going to need one."

Block Tackles.

It wasn't that she wanted something else, it was that she wanted what she once had. Anna wanted to roll back clocks, to sit in that atrium again wearing her glasses and her optimism, or even further, to the period of literature and nuance, a more academic stance against the world, before she gave it all up for the rational. She wanted to have her then-boyfriend-now-husband appear again and sit down on that bench in those jeans, have him tell her how he would change the world. Instead of saying nothing, she would have said something, maybe she would have even leaned in and kissed him, maybe she would have taken a lead. Maybe she might have said, *Let's run away together and start new.* Anna wasn't trained for risks, though. She was trained for holding back, and responding. In that way, they were absolute opposites. He was always moving forward, always eyeing goals, never letting the perfect block-tackle the good, believing. By the time she had moved toward intense interest in him, there was already a ring on her finger. And by the time she knew she was ready to take a true risk, one that involved not only her own life but the lives of others, her husband had placed them inside a life where taking risks was no longer only irresponsible, it was forbidden. Her husband had clarified what he wanted, where he was going, and how he planned to get there. There would be increasingly less space for her choices in this new arc of things. Though when it came time for her to ask for what she needed, he would not say no. He knew it would be her way out of the place she had been hiding. He knew letting her go was his insurance she would return to him.

Q.
A.

In the Salem trials, this interesting thing evolved. I call it the circular structure of the judgment. All the so-called afflicted, the ones giving the testimonies, were presumed innocent. They had seen and been abused by witches so they themselves could not be condemned. Innocent by virtue of illuminating the guilty. This structure creates all kinds of problems. It places the entire system at risk. Golden lassos.

If you're sitting overseas in a black site and a lawyer tells you it's acceptable to XYZ, who are you to say, *No, that's against the law.* Who are you to say, *I prefer not to.* An active choice to contradict a legal opinion that's in line with the mission would be arrogant, absurd, like telling the weatherman all that snow on her screen looks like clear blue skies. You follow orders in this line of work. You're not God. You're a case officer.

The only agency that grants immunity is the Justice Department, and the relationship between Justice and CIA has never been strong. Justice can blink, and change your life. At two o'clock you're on the front lines fighting ISIS in El Alamein. At three o'clock you're on an Interpol arrest list. You're placed in a windowless room and asked whether you've ever engaged in a violent plot to overthrow the U.S. government. I did something fully vetted and approved by legal counsel, the result of which was the extraction of actionable intelligence. And then Justice blinked.

I wasn't unique, this was happening all over the place, demotions framed as promotions, "rest" a wrist slap for actions they themselves had designed but could no longer tolerate.

It was clear I would be stripped of my asset.

There was no one else who could understand her, Anna.

Our chief used to say she bled red, white, and blue.

You follow orders in this line of work. On occasion, you make a choice where it's not a question of high seventies versus ice storms. It's not a question of whether to employ eyewash or what the length of your last surveillance route was, it's not about the viability of dead-drop locations, the size of the safe house, *protocol.* That's all math. When you're making a choice to save a life, the numbers evaporate and you're left with a vastly more complex thing: a human being.

Espionage isn't a math problem, Anna.

It's a painting.

Choice.

PAINT A STARRY NIGHT AGAIN, MAN.

She was trying not to think about his email. She left the bed and ordered room service. The hotel suite had started with Edmund's vision for a small, private campaign headquarters uptown. But the definition of what the suite was changed as it became the place they slept and ate, as Jake began referring to it as "home." What defines a home anyhow. She wasn't sure. She drew the curtain to see the sun starting to come up. She turned her phone off and then turned it on again. That email wasn't going anywhere until she opened it.

There's that annoying issue with the things we don't want to think about. Try not to think about pink elephants and you'll be condemned to think of nothing else. *Try not to think about starry nights, Anna,* is what she was telling herself as she moved around the suite, sitting in the chair where she had sat to answer the questions, at the little desk where she worked and watched and rewatched the boy tell his story of the rooms, lying on the daybed where she'd napped on dozens of fall afternoons, waiting for her husband to come home, the kitchen they hadn't once cooked in. It was as if she were looking for a safe space. Or for forgetting.

Of course refusing to open an email like the one sitting in her inbox would be an almost revolutionary act, an almost impossibly disciplined choice. The problem was that Anna knew one thing no one else knew. He was reaching out to her to tell her something. There would be a disclosure in that email. And perhaps there would also be an invitation. Because that night he had told her, "I will find you," and she believed him.

When you lose someone, it's almost impossible, for a period of time, to let go of the illusion that he is coming back, that he is just around the next corner, that he is about to walk into the room where you are, and turn on the light, and come to you. This is the essence of mourning.

Anna lay back down on the bed, her husband still asleep by her side.

She knew she should press delete.

You tell her I am a good man, Noel says, his voice cracking as emotion enters it.

He says this right before the video cuts out.

Tell her.

Tell who?

You tell her. You tell her that. You tell her that.

Come on, America. Loyalty.

It is better that ten guilty go free than one innocent be condemned, isn't it?

You tell her that.

At the point the video cuts out, the tiny time stamp at the bottom reads 5:32. Noel's interrogation had lasted, at that point, five hours, thirty-two minutes. And while Anna couldn't possibly guess what would come after that thirty-second minute, she could guess with some certainty who Noel meant by "you" and "her." He was talking about his daughter. He was talking about Anna. He wanted her approval. Or perhaps her forgiveness. The video was the start of something—for him, which would come back to her in time.

Anna knew she should tell someone about all of it, shouldn't she, the USB, the hard targets, fishing lessons at the Cap, now the email. She should file a report, lend testimony to the record, admit the visitation.

She had seen a witch, after all. She should confess, if only as protection.

Any other choice really wasn't appropriate.

Q.

A.

Turnover was not an option until it was the only option, funny how that works. I knew the perfect person to deliver her to, to succeed me, who would understand her history uniquely and approach the task of handling her with empathy and rigor, the one who had been assessed by the toughest critic. Her turnover would require an exfiltration, and that would solder the end of things for me. I would have to get her out, deliver her safely, and then disappear. And when I thought about this, Anna, I felt relief. I was ready. Joy needs her space.

Christmas.

Her husband always placed a piece of jewelry in the toe of her Christmas stocking. This year though, Anna wanted less. She was hopeful this year's jewel might be a poem he'd written. Maybe tickets for a trip. A gesture, an experience. Though things were busy things felt newly calm. The sprint was over and now they were in the early stages of training for the next race.

It was early December, Manhattan silent under snow, TriBeCa's glass boxes glowing through thin coats of frost. They now had two people living with them, which she felt was preposterous even as he assured her it was essential.

"It's just assistance," he told her.

"Assistance, like a chef?" she said, making air quotes around the word "assistance." She truly didn't know. He now had three assistants in his office, one who handled phones, one who handled paper, one who handled him. Her husband, who had never bothered to get his license, now had two cars equipped with two drivers. Anna felt that there were too many intrusions. As the uptown renovation continued, periodically he accused her of willfully slowing its pace, ensuring her hold on the loft as a symbol of whatever was left of their prior lives.

red, white, blue

"Not like a chef. More like a microwave," he said, lovingly, but with an edge.

The night she hung the stockings she told him, "Please don't do anything special this year."

"Only coal for you, baby." He started stepping her backward into their bedroom, a modified fox-trot, foreplay. "Key of A," he said.

Q.

A.

Noel taught me how to boil an egg. He taught me how to crack an egg, too. He could do it with one hand, as you know. One hard, swift crack, that's the trick of it. You have to come down hard enough the first time. He told me if one can crack an egg and put meat in a pan, that's enough. I still can't cook much more than eggs and a burger.

In my station, if you recruited a new source, you got a Pakistani version of the British officer's swagger stick. Inside the stick was a knife. Everyone kept these swagger sticks on their desks. And the officer with the most reports in any given month received a porcelain statue, you would place that on your desk, too. If, in the course of the year, you had the statue on your desk for the majority of the time, it meant you were the highest-ranked intelligence producer. During the years I ran her as a source, that statue just sat on my desk, it never moved. At times I would generate ten reports from one meeting with her. And when I knew it was all about to end, I took the statue into my chief's office and placed it high on a shelf. I knew he would find it after I was gone. He would know what I was trying to say.

Periodically the polygraphers would ask me about the statue. Periodically, they would question the volume of intelligence coming from one source, as if I were running ten assets and pretending it was all one person. They couldn't quite believe the truth, which was that we had struck gold in the most unlikely place. That was her blessing and her curse, the fact that she couldn't get the information out quickly enough, like I was her priest and she was coming to confess. She would sit in the safe house for five hours and not stop. I would make her eggs at three a.m. and again at six a.m. And then she would stand up and go to work, and the next week we would start all over again. I started buying more eggs. She believed what she was doing was critical to her survival. She saw her time with me as bearing witness.

Angels.

In the park, a sea of snow angels.

Looking at them, Anna thought, *I will remember this.*

Anna believed memory was an act of will. She believed the same about forgetting.

She had forgotten almost all of her Russian, and most of the novels. She had forgotten almost all of her Chinese and the maps of Asia her professor would hang on the blackboard as illustration of Asia's expanse. "Perspective," he told his students. Anna had certainly forgotten what life was like before their lives now, this pace. She'd forgotten what her mother said as Lulu removed the book from the shelf on nights when she read to her daughter, and she'd forgotten her father's response when she told him she had met the love of her life and planned to marry him. She could no longer recall her first nanny's name, or the brand of biscuits she'd loved as a child. She'd forgotten all of Noel's girlfriends, even the tall brunette who didn't care that he never wanted to marry her and wanted only to feel close to the magic everyone felt in his presence. She'd even forgotten all the boys she'd slept with at Princeton, the ones who came after the one she first loved. Anna was wrong about memory, though. Memory is not an act of will. Memory has a mind of its own.

red, white, blue

After all, as hard as she tried, Anna could not forget those men leaving the chalet that day, and she could not forget her race past the rocks at the Cap, how quietly he came up by her side. She could not forget that first fundraising dinner and the marine with his house on fire, or the former director asking if the drawing above Edmund's mantel was a Rubens. When she thought about the man who allegedly had committed crimes against his country, she could not forget the boy he had once been, rolling down the dunes, calling to the falcon. She could not forget what her husband said when she told him, the day after the election, that she needed to take a trip, a little space. To clarify, she wrapped her fingers around his wrists and said, "Microwave." He understood.

In the park the parents affirmed the art of their little angels.

Memory is as reliable as a forecast, which is to say not reliable at all. People say it rarely snows in April. People say avalanches in the Alps are on the rise. "An exceptionally icy base" was the phrase the Compagnies Républicaines de Sécurité used to describe the reasons for the unstable snowpack that season. "Even on slopes of thirty degrees," the report read, "expect instability." At that time. In those conditions. No one was making snow angels on that day in the Alps. The teams that go up the mountain looking for bodies after an avalanche know they aren't really in the rescue business.

Anna would not forget her father in the weeks before he died. His friend with the Fiat had run into trouble with the banks, and Noel was helping him negotiate with the Swiss authorities. The thing had made the papers but hadn't yet landed in court, and Noel's friend planned to try to transfer his case to another jurisdiction, a place where he could call on the European equivalent of the Fifth Amendment, and not talk. Noel thought that was a bad idea. "The

Angels.

truth will set you free," Noel told his friend. Anna asked her father if he actually believed that. "Yes," he said. "If the truth approves of your exit plan."

In the park Anna envied the children's immunity to the cold. Admiring all that white, she made a decision. When the weather turned she would return to the Cap. Walking home, she made another decision. She was going to open the email.

Q.

A.

Have you ever broken the law? Say you stole classified documents from our enemy. The answer in that case is clear, it's yes. Well what about that lollipop you slipped in your pocket that day in sixth grade, was that a crime, too? Can you recall the thoughts that led to the choice to steal the lollipop, can you recall its color or taste? Someone who arrives at a quick no on questions of memory is likely a sociopath. Sociopaths don't experience empathy, or guilt. In their minds, truth has no nuance. Their belief that they know where all the moral red lines are affords them the illusion of never having crossed one.

Yes is a mirage in the desert.

The night before the exfiltration I cooked for her in the safe house. We knew we were being listened to, so she talked about the weather and I brought water to boil, like we always had, perhaps pretending things were not about to change forever. All those nights I had placed plates of food in front of her, she had never once acknowledged it, or me; she would simply keep talking and eating and then she would stand and nod and leave. That last night was different. When I put the plate down, she stopped talking.

Q. A.

She looked up at me. I didn't move and she didn't move and after a very long pause, very slowly and clearly, she mouthed a phrase in Mandarin, not English.

Xiexie.

Thank you.

Aardwolf.

FROM: Me
TO: You
RE: Paint a Starry Night Again, Man
DATE: December 19, 2017

By those buoys.
    When it's warm.

Q.

A.

The English don't believe in the polygraph and so they don't use it. When MI6 officer Nicholas Elliott was interrogated by their equivalent of the Office of Security, he was asked whether his wife knew what he did for a living. He told the truth, which was, *Yes, she does.* The interrogators were shocked. They asked how his wife knew, and again he told the truth, which was, *Well, she was my secretary for two years and I think the penny must have dropped.* Sometimes the truth is a powerful weapon, Anna.

Nicholas Elliott was Kim Philby's closest friend. He was the one who knocked on Philby's door in Beirut after Philby had come under suspicion, after they had amassed the evidence. It was one old friend arriving to expose the other as a traitor, one friend sent specifically to indict the other as a spy. Philby had a blessed life in Lebanon, a gorgeous wife, a pet fox, fine friends; he had planned to live out his days there in the Paris of the Middle East. When Elliott arrived, Philby opened the door and said, "I knew it would be you." Occasionally you can indict a friend and also free him, Anna. The day after Nicholas Elliott arrived in Beirut, Kim Philby fled to Moscow, where he was greeted as a hero.

Breathing.

Lulu had not come for Christmas after all, though she had been open to the idea. Lulu had elected to give the happy couple the holidays in peace and so had arrived later in the dead of winter, on the coldest day of the year, in a storm. When Lulu called from the hotel, Anna told her to come to the loft, explaining that during this period of transition they were living there. Lulu held on to her daughter in the doorway long after Anna had let her own arms fall down by her side.

"You're too thin," her mother said. Lulu looked exactly the same, barely fifty at almost seventy. Those genes. "I can feel your ribs," she said.

Her mother let go and began moving through the home, investigating. Anna felt anxiety slide from her shoulder blades down along her spine. Had she emptied the sink. Was their home too spare. And all the pots lined up on the floor, the orchids in various states of distress, despite her care. Was what she was wearing acceptable. Did this look like the home of a United States senator.

Watching this woman, who was so known and also a stranger, Anna could barely remember times with her mother when she was a child. Her father was so clear. Her mother was white space. As Lulu moved from room to room, eyeing the moldings and the furniture, despairing over the orchids ("What are they doing on the floor and why are there so many of them") and opening her icebox to see shelves of Pellegrino lined up like soldiers ("Is this an installation?"), Anna closed her eyes and tried to will a memory to mind that would calm her nerves, a picture of what it once felt like to be the little girl who had a mother before her mother left. In the memory Anna was lying in her bed, around age six, eating English biscuits stolen from her nanny. Her mother was selecting a book from a shelf. It was bedtime. She could see the book's gold spine, the animals on its cover, and she could see her mother turning to her and gently removing the box of biscuits from her hold on it, placing it on the wooden nightstand. Lulu sat on the edge of her daughter's bed, smoothed the pillowcase, kissed Anna on her forehead, and opened the book—

"Christ," her mother called out from the bedroom. The intimate image in Anna's mind exploded into tiny pink hearts, emotion into cartoon. She found Lulu in her husband's closet, standing between long rows of perfectly pressed shirts hung at equal intervals, white, blue, blue, white, white, blue, black, repeat. He had more than one hundred of them, cut by tailors in London and Milan.

"Christ," Lulu repeated, and she turned to face the daughter she had not seen in more than ten years. "Does he let you breathe?"

Anna closed her eyes, and for a second and with absolute clarity she saw the girl and the biscuits and the mother and the book. And she looked at them until she was ready and then she opened her eyes and responded. "He taught me how to breathe."

Q.

A.

Did you talk to this reporter at The Washington Post? *Did you have tea in Misrata that time? Are you a spy?* Spectral evidence always says yes, Anna. There are people who never stand up and say, *This is wrong.* There are people who progress along a straight line, always asking permission, filing their reports. These are often fine people capable of accomplishing fine things. These are also the people who, with the gun cocked and while looking in the eyes of the target, will say, *Wait, what about permission?* The operating philosophy for so long at the Agency was Ask Forgiveness, Not Permission. That's an effective philosophy, Anna. Operating under that philosophy, you can imagine that on occasion by the time Headquarters sends a cable denying permission for something, no one is left in the station to receive it. That cable is a tree falling in the forest. It doesn't make a sound. I never asked for permission. And I don't need forgiveness.

Answer.

She wanted to write so many things in her response.

She wanted to say that she was stronger than she looked. She wanted to say that she hadn't minded being taken advantage of, once, on that swim, if in fact she was being taken advantage of. She wanted to say she didn't appreciate the theory she believed he was operating on, which was that she could be used in some way. She wanted to understand his intentions, why he wanted to meet her again, what he planned to tell her, was she at risk? She wanted to confront him and to scold him for not telling her more before, for perhaps setting her up for everything she'd endured over the last months. She wanted to scold and then confide in him. She wanted to tell him she was angry and afraid and felt alone. She wanted to say she had been thinking about him, and not only the him she met on her honeymoon at the Cap but also the him whose voice she heard questioning God and describing God's rooms. She had been thinking about the little boy throwing snowballs, somersaulting across sand dunes, and expressing a certainty about the world. She wanted to understand how this boy had grown up to make the choices that he did. She wanted to hear stories of Noel at another time in his life, and she wanted to know what Noel had said about her. She wanted to know if Noel's life had been lies, if the business had been real, if her own experience of her father tracked with who he actually was. She believed in the eggshells. She believed that mothers don't leave daughters so easily, and perhaps there was something to Lulu's choices she was only starting to understand. She wanted to ask to see him again because when you lose someone you love, you only want to be around people who loved him, too. She wanted to understand where the meeting place was.

She wanted to ask if he had committed crimes.

She wouldn't write anything rash.

She wouldn't write anything out of line.

She had been told not to trust him.

In the end she wrote three words, and hit send:

When is warm?

Q.

A.

We are all chasing shiny things. I was chasing impact, and impact is the real chimera, impact is anger at dirt. It's ripping out smoke alarms, it's kneeling in the grass watching dogs attack a colleague while taking no action, it's worrying the bill at the bar exceeds the system's definition of the limit. They can tell you how to deal with the idea that you might die in this line of work, but they can't tell you how to deal with the idea that you're never really living. There are stars on the wall for the deaths but there are no stars on the wall for the lives we are not living. Noel was drawn to the East because he was drawn to a certain way of thinking, the idea of letting go. He assisted in her exfiltration not because he was in love with her but because he *understood* her. And maybe because she reminded him of you. Veritas was his legacy. He saw China's future in her. If a spy steals your secrets and a hero sets you free, your father was not a spy for the Chinese, Anna. He was a hero.

He wrote his last note to me on a piece of silk, a nod to how soldiers once hid escape and evasion charts. Silk fits easily into a pocket. Silk does not dissolve in water. The silk was his way of saying, We are soldiers. His way of saying, You did it, you chose your battle, this is it.

Van Gogh.

It's so blue. Whether this reflects the artist's mood at the time of its creation is unclear, but what is clear is that the artist chose to place things on the canvas he couldn't actually see. He had studied at the feet of the realists, but he wanted to show things differently.

The artist placed the moon near the corner. Only the artist wasn't painting at night; there was not enough light for that—there was no moon. He couldn't actually observe a moon when he was painting one. Yet there is the moon. There are also buildings, signs of life, all illuminated by a moon the artist never saw. A critic later described Van Gogh as "longing for concision and grace."

It was March though still wintry in Manhattan. Anna had started going to the Museum of Modern Art afternoons, hoping to stop thinking about pink elephants by staring straight at one, by looking at the painting they had talked about that night on the Cap outside the restaurant, by processing the things that had happened since that time. The choice to paint a sky filled with stars from one's room at the asylum struck her as so sad. Anna had never liked the Post-Impressionists, not even those lilies or the lunch on the grass. Her interest in this painting had nothing to do with art.

Van Gogh.

Things were feeling chaotic lately, with Lulu now in and around the house all the time and even threatening to move to town—"to help." With her husband increasingly tied up in new civic catastrophes and in laying the groundwork for the next election. With contractors and architects and interior designers in the uptown house.

When she arrived home from the museum, it was dark and pouring. She nodded to the security guard in the hall, she was used to him now. Her mother was horrified by the presence of a man holding a gun at her door, a fact Anna felt belied Lulu's naïveté. Isn't it odd to fear a gun carried by a man sent to protect you. It was true, her mother no longer floated above. She simply stood outside. She had always seen her mother as fearless, but now increasingly experienced her fragility.

"He's there to protect me," Anna told Lulu, of the guard. "I mean, in theory."

Her husband was singing in the kitchen. His favorite album raged through state-of-the-art speakers whose value exceeded that of her engagement ring. *I went down to the demonstration / To get my fair share of abuse.* She walked in and saw the senator had made dinner, sent the assistants home. Everything was a mess. His eyes popped when he saw her, a look that still made her shy, made her miss him even in his presence. He pulled her into an old dance move, the one with the spin, then the dip. He could dance. "No, I'll get you wet," she protested, to which his response was, "Yes, please." This was not a guy who cared about staying dry. It was part of what drew people to him, it had drawn her, had complemented her fears. *Well I could tell by her bloodstained hands.* His mouth was right by her ear. He repeated the move, and the lyric. She wondered whether, if he kept holding her close, the instinct to go back to those rocks would evaporate. Though she knew it wouldn't, the instinct wasn't about him. He wouldn't send a guard with her. He believed in her. She put her hands on his face. She planned to tell him that night that she was going back to France. When the case officer responded to her email, he had told her what was warm and where was warm and when was warm. In the end they would go back to the place where they started.

Q.
A.

And you shall know the truth, and the truth shall make you free.

There's a very detailed document in the station emergency communication plan called the "reserve," or the "universal." It includes a time and place for potential re-contact with assets at some point in the future. It's used when the connection between an officer and an asset is broken or lost, usually in the wake of some catastrophe: if a war breaks out, if a bomb goes off. The location indicated in the plan is usually a wide-open space, like a park. The time indicated is highly specific, the second Saturday of each month at eleven-fifteen in the morning, for example. You know you will be going to that place at that time and if the other person is not there, you will go again the next month and the month after that and the month after that. In theory there are thousands of parks around the world right now where spies or their assets are waiting. They will return to those parks on the second Saturdays of the month with their *Financial Times* or their Falcons hats or whatever the protocols require. We call the location the "universal meeting place." An asset knows that if I ever miss a meeting, she should go there. If she keeps returning there, she knows one day I will come or I will send someone in my place to collect her and bring her home.

"And you shall know the truth and the truth shall make you free" is the Agency motto.

The Hard Verb.

What was warm? It was a code of sorts.

Noel had been buried on a hillside in Switzerland, under snow, the day after he died and the day before Anna had wrestled with that fire and those newspapers. It was hard not to think about all the history around those mountains, the images we associate with the place, edelweiss and Swiss knives and mountain dogs with whiskey barrels hung around their necks.

It had been so cold that day. It was almost evening by the time they had everything organized. Anna had gathered a tiny bouquet of edelweiss on their walk up the hill; somehow the flowers were poking through the snow. Anna and her husband and the priest stood over the grave and she placed the edelweiss. She had cried herself out. She had nothing left. She thought about setting fire to the chalet. She longed for some rash action to make it all go away.

"Don't you want him closer to you, somewhere you can check in on him?" her husband had asked, when she'd made the choice to bury Noel immediately, and there, rather than take him home.

"This is where he was happiest," she said, remembering the wedding in Klosters, the prayer flags.

Later, when he questioned the choice one last time, her response was different.

"He's here, actually," she'd said, touching her heart. "This is where he is." She said it like you say something you need to believe but for which you have absolutely no evidence.

A jeweler in Gstaad engraved a simple flat stone with the date and Noel's initials. The jeweler delivered it himself to them that day. Noel would have liked the stone. He liked to personalize things. When Lulu saw it later she liked it, too.

What was warm?

At the memorial, a month later in Manhattan, Edmund delivered the eulogy. He started out with "Noel was—" And then his voice broke. He took a pause before saying, "There it is, the hard verb." Anna always remembered that, *the hard verb. Was.* The hard verb is an idea applicable for the living, too, as we try to understand who we have been and who we are, what we might one day be.

It was April and Anna had been thinking a lot about hard verbs lately—*elected, wanted, trusted.* Interrogated. Edmund had taken her to lunch to check in and she'd deflected when he asked how she was doing. He knew exactly how she was doing, he knew her so well, he could tell she was restless. He saw restlessness as a threat.

"Is this the lunch where you make me promise not to leave until we're in the White House?" she asked, only half teasing.

"I wanted to thank you, actually, is all," he said, tucking his napkin into his collar like a child. He always ordered spaghetti with meat sauce, which wasn't on the menu, which is how you do it when you're a power player in a power player place.

"Maybe I should thank you," she said, suddenly serious.

"Have you enjoyed it *at all*?"

"Yes." And then she said, "But don't tell."

They were both thinking the same thing, which had very little to do with the senator, or politics, the race, or the candidate's future. The election really hadn't been central for either one of them but neither one of them was ready to address what had been. It was too soon.

"Public service can be exhilarating," Edmund said, doubling down on denial.

"Yes, Jackie loved it, didn't she," Anna added cooly, knowing the exact opposite to be true.

What is warm?

"Warm" is the word for the temperature of the sea along the French Riviera in June. Anna decided the choice of that word was also a play on the idea of "getting warmer," close to a solution. The French say *réchauffer* when discussing the proper preparation of a dish. It means "heat it up."

"I really think he could go all the way," Edmund said. He was looking down at his bowl. He scraped his bread against its edge to catch the sauce.

"Yes, he probably could. He has it all, right?"

"When you got engaged I told Noel I thought he was a criminal. A very charming criminal."

Noel, Noel, Noel.

.   .   .

"You didn't like the drugs."

Edmund put down his fork, cleaned his mouth. He took a sip of water. He looked out the window.

"What is it?" Anna said. "Tell me."

"They found him."

"What do you mean, they found him."

"You never heard from him again, right?"

Anna didn't answer.

"Well, it doesn't matter anymore. They found him, they had a talk with him, they got what they wanted. It's over."

Anna wondered if the word "talk" was a euphemism.

"Where is he now," she said, thinking about the koans and the things that can't be said.

Edmund looked at her, this girl who had suffered enough, in his view, who had effectively lost her mother and later buried her father, who had given up a career for her husband and who had been unable to have a child. Under all the privilege, she had fought wars, too. He reached down and opened his briefcase. He handed her a manuscript. On the cover was the letter *A*.

"What's this," she said.

"Homework. Or perhaps, history."

Edmund had read it. He had left it almost intact. He had edited out only one page, the answer to a question about Noel's dying friend, in that hospital in that city the night Anna was born. The answer detailed Noel's ambivalence about becoming a father, and implied this was the real reason he wasn't home that night, how even the most complex work pales in complexity when up against intimacy. Thrill, mission, and risk were also what Noel once wanted. Edmund didn't see his decision as a sin of omission, he saw it as a mercy blow. Sometimes you don't want the whole story, was his view. Like Increase Mather, he was entitled to one.

"These are only answers," she said, flipping pages. "Where are the questions."

"Homework," he repeated, quietly.

She read the first sentence out loud.

" 'Espionage is not a math problem.' What does it mean."

He paused and set his eyes on hers then said, "It means you're old enough now."

The most powerful interrogation is the one we perform on ourselves.

Q.

A.

Noel was an artist underneath it all, Anna, you know that. You knew the poet before you knew the rest. We all knew the poet, too. And we accepted the rest. We looked at Noel as an eccentric and a rebel, immune to rule, often infuriatingly iconoclastic. But he was our eccentric, our rebel, a bridge to the magic past of China Ops but never prisoner to all that, the guy who got out, who walked away from the mission when the mission no longer had meaning for him. Noel was open to wonder and doubt. In the end he would visit infrequently. We would talk about imminent threats or local upcoming elections and Noel would quote Martin Rees, the British cosmologist. He would remind the young guys that Rees had honorary degrees from Oxford, Yale, Toronto, Durham, Trinity College, and then he would tell us how Rees didn't write about imminent threats or upcoming elections, he wrote about the viability of life on other planets. "There is a lot more life out there than we could ever detect," was a line Noel loved. It was his way of reminding us we would never wrap our minds around it all, his way of reminding us to remember higher things, the big decisions, not the little ones. We were in London, at a bar, when I told him what I was going to do with Veritas. He took a long pause then said, "Hey, there is a lot more life out there." This response was his way of saying he understood. He was giving me permission—and forgiveness. I guess in the end I needed it after all.

Sweet Virginia.

End of June, Anna flew to Nice. Air France, a window seat, the business-class ticket a gift from the senator. She hadn't flown alone in years and it made her nervous, no hand to hold on taking off, no one to fall into with exhaustion on arrival. Nothing is happening here, she told herself. Nothing is changing, nothing is at risk. All that was happening on that plane was that a woman was taking three days away from her life to figure something out. The fact that she might be taking three days to live her life never occurred to her.

The answers told the story of a life in a certain line of work at one point in time. Anna read them and she now knew what had happened that day in Switzerland and she understood what had happened before. She'd shared the answers with her husband and he had said, "You have to go and find him." She'd offered to share them with her mother but her mother didn't want to read them. In the end Lulu didn't really want clarity about Noel. She had made her choices, he would never be a hero in her eyes.

As the plane descended, the man next to Anna leaned over to lift the blind. The sky was clear. "Bienvenue," he said. She was thinking, *Are you waiting for Sweet Virginia? Yes, my name is Ron Wood.*

Q.

A.

A thousand tourists can't really reconstruct a beach, Anna. You can collect ten million grains of sand, but by the time you've excavated the beach, there's a new beach in its place. The idea behind the thousand-grains-of-sand philosophy isn't about some special attention to detail. The idea is about people. That's China's true comparative advantage—people. When you consider human beings an unlimited resource, you might begin to underestimate the value of one life.

Collecting intelligence is the art of letting go. Espionage is blind faith.

Not long after we met, Noel and I ended up at a funeral. I stayed after the service to pray and when I turned to leave, the chapel had emptied out and only Noel stood at the back, waiting for me. He was fascinated to learn that I was religious. He asked if I believed in Heaven, and that was when I told him about the rooms, this idea I'd had as a little boy. I don't even know where it came from, maybe a photograph, maybe a book, maybe an ad on TV. Later, he told me he shared it with you, "that it was just too good," he said. Though typically, he made it better. He made it brighter. He told me about the glass trellis and the courtyard, about joy. The care he took with the image of Heaven's rooms was the care he took with everything, Anna. Your father took a vision and made it his own.

Now when I think about Noel, I see him in those rooms. I see him walking that courtyard, and admiring that flowered glass trellis. I imagine him directing the angels as to where they need to take more care, I imagine him calling in the landscape architects and the English gardeners, the specialists for old edifices in need of repair. For him there are mountains in those rooms, too, peaks to make the Matterhorn blush, fresh tracks for days. Close your eyes and see if you can see him like this. See if you can see your father in a place where they are no longer watching or listening, where there is no more pressure to perform. They were always watching, Anna. Noel knew there would be one day when some old friend walked through the door and asked him to answer for a choice he'd once made, maybe in that jail, maybe later, maybe in the little white house at Langley or on Park Avenue or Bond Street or in Shanghai or Zurich. I believe whatever happened on that mountain other than the intersection of weather and human error, of chance and probability, doesn't matter. I believe in the moment it happened he didn't fight it.

There is one room I never told him about. It's not one I envisioned as a boy.

It's the room for forgiveness.

In this room, they wash you clean. In this room, they understand means and ends, theory and practice, good and evil. In this room you can know finally and with certainty that there is a God. The room for forgiveness is the room for belief.

Belief isn't a coin flip at the circus, Anna. It's a feeling.

The body knows, the body never lies.

You can feel belief like you can feel the sun.

I see it all so clearly now.

Q. A.

Yes, it's extraordinary.
Yes, it's true.
Heaven.
This.

blue

What's blind about blind faith?

That's what Anna was thinking as she hit the water.

If faith is defined as belief in the absence of proof, isn't all faith blind?

When she dove into the sea it was cold. A quarter-mile from shore there's a line of white buoys to mark the limits of the lifeguards' view. Anna swam past the buoys, and kept on. She was thinking about the universal meeting place. Place*s*. *Bali, Beijing, Jakarta. Rome, Saigon, Damascus. Manhattan, TriBeCa, Moore Street, Number Nine. Past the lacquered pots, through the kitchen, in the bedroom.* Your only goal is to arrive and be patient and believe the other person will arrive, too.

There is a blind faith in that.

"This is a fine universal meeting place," was what he'd said that afternoon, standing on the rocks before that first swim, before she said "provincial" and dove in.

"'Universal meeting place' sounds cult*ish*," she told him.

"Yes, cult, exactly. The idea was developed in a kind of cult."

*

An elevated heartbeat skews a poly.

And even an expert can cause an avalanche.

When the polygraphers traveled to the house in the Alps, despite the existence of an embassy in town, Noel was solicitous, his specialty. He even went to collect them himself from the plane. There were two technicians and there was also the deputy director of operations, an old friend, perhaps sent along to smooth things. As the men drove up in altitude, the temperature dropped. Noel told stories. He shared how he had once spent a holiday there as a child. He pointed out the steep, central couloir and said, "We ski it with torches, New Year's Eve." He told the men he found the air, and the women, to be more beautiful there than anywhere in the world. Out their windows they saw stands of fresh strawberries, yes even in winter. Noel insisted they stop and try some. The polygraphers had never been treated like this and seemed disarmed.

At the chalet, Noel showed them around and led them out to a wide, wood porch. It was covered with ice. "Don't slip," he said. He offered an early lunch and more stories before directing the technicians into a small study. He took the third man into an adjacent bedroom and suggested, perhaps ironically, a nap, before looking right at him and saying, "I knew it'd be you." Noel noted that his soon-to-be-son-in-law was expected home soon; that he'd gone into Geneva to get the rings, that his daughter would be married the next day. Though Noel well knew these men were not there to discuss rings or weather conditions. They were not there to hear his happy memories. They had not come all the way from northern Virginia for fresh strawberries, for sliced figs and raclette. They were there to ask about the young case officer. The one who had been ordered home a year before after conducting an enhanced interrogation somewhere in Indonesia, but who instead of coming home had then participated in the exfiltration of an asset he'd inherited from Noel.

Noel knew all this. And so before the machine was even turned on, as they were preparing, he told the men the person they'd come to discuss was a good man. He said that to lose such a man and the knowledge he'd accrued in Asia was not acceptable. He told them about first meeting the officer in the little white house at Langley. He told them how everyone had been struck by this kid of Scotch-German descent who spoke perfect Russian and Chinese, who was devoutly religious and also very witty, and kind. And who was unmarried, and seemed uninterested in love. "Which of course is the ultimate defense," he told them as they prepared the machine. "It's not a pen dipped in poison that protects us, is it. It's emotional control." He said that losing a man like that would pose a risk to national security.

This was the second pistol in a way. Inciting fear about risks to national security was philosophical insurance. When you incite fear about national security you insure your point of view. "He's not a spy," Noel told them, re-laying the first pistol as he had in myriad conversations throughout preceding days. Now he would be tested on that view. Now he would tell it to the machine. "He did nothing wrong," he told them, convincing himself even as he said it, like Anna placing her hand on her heart.

And yet the needle had skipped on Noel's answer. Despite his training in how to control his breath. Despite the stories and the charm. Despite his conviction he would sail through this formality and emerge having saved another life. When the needle skipped, the more senior of the two technicians said simply, "Would you like to try again?"

He was one of the Agency's finest. His technical skills and emotional intelligence exceeded the stereotypes he himself acknowledged as often true of people in his line of work. He hadn't swallowed Noel's charm or his stories or the strawberries or the view. All that grandeur, if anything, appalled him. The tradition he knew Noel represented. And what especially appalled him was what he understood of why he was there. People had been placed at risk for one young officer's whim. He believed that young officer had committed crimes even before the exfiltration. He believed most case officers were morally unmoored, that they got high off preying on the weak. He believed rogues and elitists required slaps on their wrists. He had flown all this way to perform his job and had an idea of the ideal outcome. So he made a remark, casually, right before turning on the machine. He knew exactly what he was doing. He was throwing Noel off his game. The remark was about the Chinese girl.

An elevated heartbeat skews a poly.

Even an expert—

Would you like to try again?

That was when Noel stood up, tore off the wires. That was when he walked out of the room, went downstairs to strap on his skins and take his skis. There was still time for last runs, the sun wouldn't set for hours, lifts were open, snow was fresh.

The deputy director of operations later told the technicians to pack up their things, that they would drive to Geneva the next day and do it properly, at the embassy.

And they would have, but the next day Noel was dead.

The last thing he did before he headed up the mountain was load the pistol, a tiny Sig he kept locked in the top drawer of his desk. The Swiss rescue would find it later, in the snow, the chamber empty. Noel hadn't taken the pistol for protection, or suicide; that was never the plan. Was the plan to fire rounds in the air, speed the shifting of the snow? Though what if the shots fired didn't make a sound? The rescue team also found a state-of-the-art silencer, one that fit the pistol perfectly. Typically Swiss, they reported this all to the police, who reported it to the embassy, which is to say to the Agency. The ambassador assured Anna the cause of death was asphyxiation. "Doesn't hurt a bit," he said. He was half-Austrian and had lost his own father in an avalanche in St. Anton. Surfeit of honey, surfeit of snow.

*

There exists, however, a God.

As Anna swam out, she was waiting for the water to feel warm, her cue to return. She knew he would be there for her. They would tell stories about her father and she would not ask about interrogations or asset exfiltrations, about the rise of China or elements of tradecraft; she would ask about God's rooms, about the compass and the falcon, about the safe-house keeper. This would be her closure, a bell to end the mourning; it was time to end it. And yet as she thought about that bell and about what she would ask—*wait, what?*—something suddenly made no sense. She had met him before, of course. She had seen the video and she had been shown, by the interrogators, the photograph of him in the hospital, the one they'd placed on the table in the hotel. She would know him immediately. Why had he given her the parole? Why did she need to know about Sweet Virginia?

That night, under those stars in France, he had told her, *When you walk away from the Agency, you walk away from that life. It is not a job, it is a way of life.* He told her, *The culture of the Agency is unique and bizarre. When you rejoin the world after you leave, the adjustment*

period is actually quite significant. When he identified the rocks by
that sea as the "universal meeting place," he knew she would return
when the time came. She was easy to spot and assess, she was simply a girl who had lost her father. When they met, she was seeking a
way back from that loss. He was seeking a way back, too. And what
she said that night outside the restaurant showed him the way. She
said, *When you lose someone you love, you only want to be around the
people who loved him, too.*

*

If he was alone on the mountain that day, Noel would have been
ecstatic, and calm. He used to say there was no quiet like the one
at last tracks, that near-end-of-the-day when the light changes.
If he was alone and if he triggered the avalanche he would have
responded with calm, perhaps even with amusement, he always
had a sense things happen for a reason, that timing is a thing we
can swat at but never quite catch, a butterfly. He would perhaps
have had last thoughts about his legacy, about the one or two lives
he had touched and altered, about a little girl and eggshells. He
would have seen and heard lines from the poets he loved. As the
snow came down he would have listened to the poets, not the fear.

*

On the beach Anna shook the water from her hair and closed her
eyes. When she opened them she looked up at the rocks. And there,
looking back at her, was a woman she immediately recognized. The
hard target, the girl in the flowered blue silk dress, up late in a safe
house, the future, Veritas. This was her closure, her bell. This was
the reason for the parole, the transcript of answers, the video, this
was the reason Noel had stood up and torn off the wires and why a

gifted young officer had disappeared. This was the end of a story of risks and choices. *This, she.* This was her turnover.

Anna said nothing and didn't move. As she looked up at those rocks though, the moat began to empty and the drawbridge prepared to descend. The terror of a loss receded, making room for something new in its place. In that moment, she believed. She finally believed.

Oh, my soul. Let me be in you now. Look out through my eyes.
Look out at the things you made. All things shining.

—TERRENCE MALICK

Acknowledgments

Sonny Mehta, Eric Simonoff, and Shelley Wanger.
Carroll Carpenter. Elliot Ackerman, "standing on the balcony
railing, holding the universe together." And Vail & Alexis,
who listen to my stories every night and especially love ones
with knights in shining armor.

*

Ed Victor
(1939–2017)

Author's Note

This is a work of fiction. No one I interviewed during the course of my research disclosed classified information.

A NOTE ABOUT THE AUTHOR

Lea Carpenter lives in New York with her two sons.

A NOTE ON THE TYPE

This book was set in Adobe Garamond.

Composed by North Market Street Graphics,
Lancaster, Pennsylvania

Printed and bound by Berryville Graphics,
Berryville, Virginia

Designed by Soonyoung Kwon